THE HERALD

Also by *Michael Shaara:*

THE BROKEN PLACE
THE KILLER ANGELS
(awarded the Pulitzer Prize)

THE
HERALD

MICHAEL
SHAARA

McGRAW-HILL BOOK COMPANY

New York   St. Louis
San Francisco
Hamburg   Mexico   Toronto

1 2 3 4 5 6 7 8 9 DODO 8 7 6 5 4 3 2 1

LIBRARY OF CONGRESS CATALOGING IN PUBLICATION DATA
Shaara, Michael.
The herald.
I. Title.
PS3569.H2H4   813'.54   80–27495
ISBN 0–07–056376–4

Book design by Roberta Rezk.

What causes a species to disappear . . . is the profitable "invention" that falls by chance to one or a few of its members in the everlasting gamble of hereditary change.
—KONRAD LORENZ

Now, my suspicion is that the universe is not only queerer than we suppose, but queerer than we can *suppose. . . . I suspect there are more things on heaven and earth than are dreamed of in* any *philosophy.*
—J. B. S. HALDANE

To my father: Thank you, Pop

ONE

The night air above nine thousand feet was black and cold and very smooth. He put the nose of the plane down and began to gather speed. The girl slept, head against the far window. He smiled, patted the splendid thigh, flushed hot exhausted memories: dreamed. Marvelous few days with that girl. Again? He trimmed the plane to go down hands off. *Lord, 'tis black.* He was above all the haze, high over the smoke, thundering along in cold black springwater air. There were high clouds blotting the stars and very few lights down under the haze below, and no moon. He was flying over swamp-and-hammock country, far from the cities to the north, and the haze of smoky air cut out all forward vision. The only lights he saw were the dim fuzzy sparks below him gliding by in the dark like boatlights in a fog. To the left was the vast black of the ocean at night: the Gulf. He searched out there for a boatlight and saw nothing, nothing at all, and felt the cool chill of wonder: all that darkness, all that rolling sea. Will fly across it someday. Feel some of what they felt, the early men, Lindbergh and the rest.

The engine seemed rough. It roared; he listened. He thought: imagination? But if it quits *now* . . . a long way down . . . in whistling silence. They all say: "Don't fly at night." But in the night, ah, 'tis calm and smooth. You're all alone. In clean air. And if it quits . . . it quits. Don't think on that. But if it quits . . . we'll come down in the trees. But it won't quit. I've been over it every inch. Old airplane. Found junked, wing all bent where some idiot did the prang, prop like gray spaghetti. Ah: I have a gift for this. He patted the dash tenderly, fondled the ancient wheel. With my own hands I made you. Beautiful bird. And so is *she*. He touched the girl, moved his hand along the warm soft leg, under the soft cloth of the dress.

He began to pick up the glow that was Jefferson. It shone under the haze, down the horizon, like a white distant fire. Still a long way off. Amazing how far you could see, above the haze. The smog lay flat, like a lake, and in the day you rose slowly above it into the clear blue. The line was definite, and it was astounding how clear the air was just above that line: once above the line you could see forever. Now he must go down. Not yet, not yet. The glow enlarged. Must have a tail wind. He checked: ground speed very good. He began to let down. Careful, don't let the airspeed build. He trimmed for descent. Come down slowly: you'll hurt her ears. He remembered yesterday, flying south. He had been between two layers of cloud, one of those few magnificent times so beautiful you never forget, merely have to close your eyes to see them: clouds below, a great gray ocean, clouds above, flat ceiling. You felt detached from the earth and suddenly it was as if you were coming down on another planet, and there beneath the clouds, when you got down, you would find something wholly strange, something different and dangerous and unbelievable. But going along between the two layers of cloud there was no earth and no blue sky, only the cloud, and he thought: *this* is what they'll feel going down on Venus, if they ever go down, if they can muster the curiosity. He shook his head. They are losing the curiosity. They don't care about Venus.

The girl stirred. Changing pressure was affecting her ears. He was down to five thousand, coming down into the haze. He could pick out the green-flashing beacon of Jefferson Airport. He tuned in Jefferson Approach Control

4

and called in. There was no answer. He called again. No answer. He looked at the clock: 5:10 A.M. Asleep at the switch. He did not feel at all sleepy, just a bit tired, pleasantly tired. The perfume of the girl was sweet in the cabin air. He called again.

Silence.

He was down to three thousand. Coming down fast. He raised the nose to slow the descent. He thought: my radio was working fine when I took off. He changed frequencies, tried again, again there was nothing. The lights of the town were beginning to glide by beneath him. He saw the twin headlights of a lone truck moving along the truck route that circled the town. He thought, *this is damned strange*. He called. A voice answered: "Stinson 33 Kilo. This is Eastern 287. I'm circling above you. How do you read?"

He dropped a wing, looked up. A big jet, invisible in the body but glittering with strobes and a red light. He answered. The cool Eastern voice came back:

"I heard your call. I've been trying to get *somebody*, but they don't answer on any frequency. I'm in contact with Jacksonville; they're trying to get through by phone. Probably a power failure. If you'll hang on, I'll pass the word."

The Eastern jet was the early morning flight up from Miami, through to Atlanta. He turned toward it, keeping it visible above him, in front of him. Power failure? But all the lights down there were blazing away. He thanked the jet, began to move in over the field. To the jet he said, "I'm in the landing pattern. Everything looks fine."

"Right. Going to land?"

"Negative. Think I'll circle a bit."

"Jacksonville doesn't get an answer. They say the phone is dead."

"I see cars moving down there."

After a moment Eastern said, "Interesting."

"Charming."

5

He floated along above the path of landing lights. He had absolutely no idea what could be wrong. Eastern said, "We've called the Air Force. There'll be a few jets here, in a little bit."

"Right." He turned automatically onto a natural base leg, the plane sinking slowly toward the silent earth. He said, "Runway looks clear."

"Are you going down?"

"I think I'll drag it once, for a look."

"Right. I'll keep an eye on you. But it ain't easy to circle this thing. What kind of a Stinson is that?"

"Voyager 108." He was turning on final approach, beginning to be busy, holding the runway in front of him: the two lines of narrow path. He backed off on the power. In the softer sound the girl began to stir. But he was very busy. He could see bright lights everywhere and the green towers flashing, a truck out on the highway, all perfectly normal. He came in over the edge of the runway, flew slowly along a few feet in the air, down the white centerline, flew the whole length of the runway, and then pushed in the power and rose up again into the black. The girl said, "Nick?"

He explained. He looked for the big jet: it was banking in the south. He said, "It looks fine. I can't figure it."

There was a moment of silence. To Rachel he said, "You know, honey? This is damned weird." Eastern said, "I'm using too much fuel. Got to move on. Can't land here without permission; so guess I'll go to Albany." After a moment, formally, "What are your intentions?"

"I don't have the fuel for Albany and . . . nothing else is lighted."

He was turning downwind along the runway. The runway seemed safe. Eastern said, "Are you going down?"

"Think I will."

"Roger. Want me to wait a bit? The Air Force types will be here any minute."

"Appreciate it." He flew downwind, cut the power once more, turned slowly on base, dropping a wing into the dark. He felt suddenly very nervous. It was not easy to put the ancient bird down, and he needed concentration. Eastern said, "Used to fly a Stinson once, long time ago. Good bird."

Nick came in low and slow. He put the big flaps down, and the plane hung in the air. He held power and touched gently, holding her off a long moment as she slowed, feeling her grow heavy, heavy, felt the tail come down, the weight settle, slowing, the runway fine and smooth and endless, no problem. He was down; he taxied off the runway into a lane of blue lights. Nothing moved. He said, into the radio, "No sweat, Eastern. Everything is fine."

"Do you see anybody?"

He taxied slowly toward the tower. No motion anywhere. The girl was staring foggily, blinking. She would be patient while the men talked. Nick said, "Nobody here."

Eastern said, with obvious regret, "Got to be moving on. Sorry. Listen, what's your name?"

"Tesla. Nick Tesla."

"Right. Well, you sit tight and the Air Force will be there in no time. If you have any trouble get right on frequency 121.5. Everybody will be listening. Right. Well, see you. Wish I could hang around."

Nick Tesla watched the jet go, rising toward the north. He was not afraid; he had not had time for fear. As he taxied toward the tower he was aware of the growing silence, and when he pulled up by the tower and cut the engine the sound of that died a sudden death and the silence was stunning. The girl said, "But where *is* everybody?"

Nick got out of the plane. He looked up at the green beacon rotating above the silent tower. He could see soft lights in the tower ceiling but no motion. Normally when you landed here there was a gas truck out to meet you, but now there was no one. He saw the gas trucks parked over by the hangar, one yellow light burning calmly in the office. He said, "This is creepy."

The girl came around the plane and held his arm. He said, "It can't be just the radio. They have more than one radio. And they have auxiliary power. And the lights are on. Damn." He felt a rising chill. The door of the tower building was open: bright yellow light within. Until now he had been just curious; now he was suddenly animal wary. He could feel disaster like a coming ghost. But out on the highway a truck roared by, normal sound of a normal night. He said, "Got to look."

He was thinking: ought to gas up and get out of here. But first, must find out what's happening. Curiosity overwhelmed the fear. He walked toward the control tower. The girl followed, holding his arm. She was very small, with round black eyes. They went in to the FAA Station.

There was no one on the first floor. All the lights were burning. A teletype clicked: another, in the next room. He thought: *incredible.* There was a drawing on a Plasticine sheet, in blue crayon, of a weather pattern. In the lower-right-hand corner was marked, in red crayon: "2 A.M." The girl said, "Where do you suppose they went?"

He shook his head. There had to be *someone* here. He walked through the FAA quarters into the weather bureau office. Again, no one. Everything neat, everything tidy, no sign of trouble. He thought: *Christ, they're all gone.* But there were cars moving on the truck route. Memory of that reassuring. On the far side of the weather bureau office were stairs leading to the tower, but he did not bother to go up. He called, "Anybody home?" knowing he would get no answer and feeling at the moment he spoke an odd sense of violation of the silence, as if you ought to be quiet, in all the quiet. Rachel held his arm.

He was thinking: *gas up the plane and get the hell out of here.*

He longed to be up in the clean air. Still very dark outside. No light for at least an hour. He said, "Wait here a moment."

"The hell I will. Where are you going?"

"Thought I'd check the men's room."

"Well, all right. But I'm coming right along."

He opened the door, saw: a pool of vomit. He smelled it. He told her to stand there, holding the door open. There was a man in one of the stalls. Gray cheeks. Dead. He had apparently vomited before he died. Nick recognized the face: Joe Warner. Old poker buff. Nick felt a trickle of nausea; shoved it off. The girl was holding her throat.

"Is he sick?"

Nick shook his head. That's where the rest of them are. They sit somewhere . . . in pools of vomit. Jesus. Only one man on night duty in FAA. But where's the one in the weather bureau? Jesus. They can't *all* be . . . trucks moving out on the highway. Nick said, "Let's go."

"But what's the matter with him?"

"He's dead. Come on." He went out, tugging her arm. Nick looked toward the main building, toward the gas truck, walked that way. He was becoming scared. Before he reached the truck he could smell vomit. He looked in the window of the little office. Man was on a chair, draped there, piece of meat. Nick backed off. Vomit. Plague? The Black Death. Christ, what have I touched?

Rachel saw the body. She believed. Nick said, "Let's gas up. Let's get out."

He started to get into the gas truck. But on the road out there a truck roared by. Plague might be just *here*. Only here. Get into town: to the hospital. His car was parked by the hangar. He went.

She was silent. She took his hand. She said, "They're dead. They're all dead."

He started his car. She sat in the corner.

"A disease?" she said. "Are there bugs in the air?"

9

"Who the hell knows?" He twitched. "Christ, isn't this something? I think we ought to head for the hospital." He thought: if it's a plague, bet we've already got it. Memories of warnings came to his brain, a battery of scientists with windy language: *there will either be plague or war, plague on a scale undreamed of* . . . but what about those trucks out there? The airport. Plague starts at the airport. Did somebody land here today? And if so, and if they brought it into the airport, isn't it the worst thing you could do to go into town, carrying it with you? But God only knows. It's already in town. He turned out on the truck route but there were no trucks now, no lovely oily diesel stench. But the lights of town shone steadily ahead, a red light blinked; he waited legally patiently for it to turn, the first fear beginning to die: you've got it, whatever it is, got it already.

He drove into town. The girl was silent. They passed no cars. There was no motion anywhere. It was a small town and there were only a few places open all night, and when he passed one of them the light was shining inside; the counter was lighted and he could see cups of coffee along a glassy counter. He swerved abruptly and turned in. Somebody should be here. He got out of the car and opened the door and there was the smell of vomit. He told her to stay in the car. Now he was truly scared. But he went into the cafe and looked beyond the counter, and the waitress lay there. He was a nighttime person and he had known her. Name was Cora: cheerful, slow, very bad teeth. He went back outside. The round black eyes of the lovely girl in the car stared back like black diamonds. He said, "I think . . . we ought to get to the hospital."

He touched the car and felt a shock. Not a bad shock, but he pulled his hand away. And the shock was still there. It ran all through him, a tingle all over his body like warm electricity. For one long eerie second he thought he was going crazy and the feeling was the nerve endings beginning to come apart, but the shock persisted and was not bad and he had the sensation that he was standing in a low-grade electric current. He was thinking: something must have failed somewhere. Then he saw lights moving. A car was coming. He stepped out onto the road. The driver of the car saw him and swerved toward him and stopped. A police car. Nick thought, somebody alive. Thank God. A big round man got out, shone a flashlight in his face. Sheriff. Nick did not know him.

The big man said, "What's going on? What's happening?" His voice was husky and squeaky, and he was breathing very hard. He was scared. There was another man in the car, a deputy. He opened the door and stood behind it, leaning on it.

Nick said, "I don't know. I just flew into the airport. There's a dead man out there. Cora's dead"—he pointed —"in there. Do you believe it? My God, what's going on?"

The Sheriff said, "I can't find nobody." He was not in control, he was whining, his eyes were sick. "I got a call to come up here, over the phone, and I got here and they're dead. I haven't . . . this is . . ." He stopped talking, stood paralyzed, helpless. He said, "Some kind of plot. We ought to . . ."

"Get to the hospital, that's where I'm going."

"George?" The deputy spoke in a sick voice, leaning against the door of the car. "George? I don't feel so good."

The Sheriff turned. "I'm getting the hell out of here." He got back into the car, turned, shrieked off. A few feet off he turned the siren on and the blue light on and screamed away from there, blinking and burning, although there was nothing moving anywhere, nothing at all.

Now Nick felt a peculiar paralysis. The electric current was still there. He felt an enormous helplessness. He got back into the car and sat there numb, unable to think. After a moment Rachel said, "Nick?"

11

He turned, slowly. He saw the eyes in a shadowed face. Look of pain.

"Nick, I feel awful."

The knowledge opened like a black door. She said, "I'm going to be sick."

He touched her arm. He said, "I'll get you out of here."

He started the car, drove to the hospital. All the lights were blazing brightly; beyond the hospital was the first glow of morning. He stopped at the front door and helped her up the steps, but he opened the door to silence and the sick smell of vomit. He came back down the steps. Now he was sick himself. He was thinking, what's the point? But he had to keep moving. It was all sick, everywhere. Had to get away from here, up in the clean air. He put her in the car and drove toward the airport. He heard a great noise: three jets passed overhead, flying low, circling to land. He could see the morning coming, gray and wet and cool. He reached the airport as the jets were taxiing in. He rode out toward them, waving them away. He tried to tell them there was plague here, not to come in. He stopped by the first jet: beautiful thing, colorful, deadly, so fast and sleek and wet in the morning. The pilot got out but put on his oxygen mask. Nick explained. The pilot nodded, got on the radio for instruction. Nick ran back to the car.

She was dead. She had died while he was gone. He opened the door and knelt there, checking her pulse, the throat. She was dead. No motion in the flesh. A little girl: her mouth open. She was dead. He put his head down against her knee.

But it was all too soon. He had not known her long. He felt no pain. Emptiness was spreading through him like a vacant fog. He thought: soon now, *you'll* die. The words meant nothing. The girl was: asleep. He searched for the sickness in his belly. It was coming. He knelt by the car, and in a few moments the jets were gone, lifting with the huge and brutal thrust in to the gray wall of the morning. He knelt and looked again. Rachel was dead. Warm. Still. He rose and walked over and sat on a cement post and waited, watching the morning come. He could hear the morning dew falling from the eaves of the building. Then he went back and lifted her out of the car and carried her into the office and laid her on the couch. He sat there for a while looking at her, and then it was fully light and he was still able to move. He thought: she is smaller; it got to her more quickly. He wondered how much time there was. He went back to his car and started it and began driving slowly toward home, waiting, feeling the sickness flooding his belly. There was no one at home that he loved. He did not seem to feel anything. Everything was suspended while he waited to die. Curious. Would not have expected it. He drove past the steaming lake, superbly beautiful in the gray and deadly morning, and he saw the first movement: a dog wandering in the mist along the lakeshore. He thought: *it doesn't get dogs,* and then up the dirt road by the lake he saw a human form: dark thin body, young boy, black boy, and the boy saw his car coming and ran away into the brush.

Someone still alive. Some take longer to die. Oh, God. Maybe some are immune. He turned and drove toward the heart of dawn. Now it was full day and there should have been people, but the streets were empty and the night lights still flashed feebly, blinking. He stopped at the corner of Main and College and looked down the hill at the incredible gray world. Nothing. No one. Streets empty and still as if all the world was a photograph. He cut the engine, and the silence came. He sat waiting. He was feeling very strange, pushed by pressure inside, not yet afraid of death but still afraid of a force loose inside him, bewildered, exploding. Were they *all* dead? And he did not miss them. There was no

13

one in the whole town to miss. He shook his head. There is no one in the town I loved. Strange and sad. In all my life, I loved airplanes. And women.

He did not know how to prepare. He expected momentary death. He thought: you'll know it's coming when you begin to throw up. But the stubborn stomach felt imaginary pain, then nothing. He became aware slowly of a most eerie appalling sensation. He did not know what it was. He got out of the car, his nerves tingling. A strangeness in the air all about him. For the first time he began to wonder if perhaps he was going mad. What a god-awful feeling. He listened.

What he was hearing was the enormous *silence*. In the far distance, a single bird. He waited, and there was a sound like water in his ears, a peculiar ringing, then a strange, stretching, crackling sound that he realized suddenly was the cracking of his own belt as he breathed. He had never heard such silence. The silence of *no one*, of no one at all, no one anywhere in all the brick houses. No one on asphalt streets. No breathing. No speech. No horns, no sound of tires on pavements, no ringing phones, no click of typewriters, no sound of anything human at all, only that one bird, in the far distance, on one desolate tree. And he could hear his own breath, in the heart of town. He got back in the car and started the engine; it leaped to life with a metallic purr, robotic and dead. He drove home.

I may live. I may be immune. Don't hope yet. What to do? Oh, God, I have to wait.

He lived in a house near the lake, near the airport. A house left by dead parents. He had always liked to be alone. The world he moved through was like a dream from his youth: he remembered it now, dreaming that he was alone; no one anywhere in all the wide world. He thought: must be crazy. Cannot be happening. Rachel? He went inside the house and made himself a cup of coffee, which was the only thing to do, and came back out on the porch and sat there looking down at the lake trying to trace it back, to see where he'd gone crazy. But it was all perfectly common and rational until he came within sight of the glow of Jefferson and called them on the radio, and then it was all mad. Rachel couldn't be dead. He sat on the porch and drank the coffee. Lights still worked. Everything fine, so far. God, interesting nightmare. Yet, I don't feel like I'm dying. The radio—

He jumped to the television set, turned it on. Long dark moment. The local station was not on the air; of course not. But—*can this be happening to the whole world?* He switched channels. It had never occurred to him—how can you think clearly when it is all crazy—but there was a face on channel 10, Albany, news bulletin.

The world focused into a stunning clarity. A thin-faced newsman with haggard eyes, reading a white paper: ". . . could not be reached for comment. But sources close to the Governor said he was in touch with the White House and would shortly make a statement. Meanwhile reports continue to be received from surrounding areas. A number of persons in the area are apparently still alive. Contact has been made by telephone with at least three persons in the area whose names have been withheld. Just how many people have survived in the county is not known at this time. There is no doubt, however, that Jefferson County is a major disaster area, and all people are warned again, I repeat, to stay away from the area."

The man went on speaking, warning people to stay out of Jefferson County. Roadblocks had already been set up. A highway patrolman appeared, with a map, pointing to roads that had been closed. Nick watched, huddled in bleary fascination. The newsman came back again, face strained, eyes showing some sign of fear, to say that the area had not yet been quarantined, but in view of the mounting evidence that the disaster may have been a contagious disease all persons were warned not only to stay out of the area but to report anyone seen entering or leaving it. The newsman read from papers handed to him. Then abruptly he was off the air, and there was a videotape of an exercise program. Nick Tesla sat staring, unmoving. In the eye of the storm. They don't know I'm alive.

Must be disease. Or germ warfare? Shipment came through town and blew up. Nerve gas. Most likely. God-damned Army.

The news was back, but he learned little. It came in fragments. A terrible thing was happening. No one knew why. He sat in front of the set, drinking coffee. It did not occur to him to call anybody. He had no one to call. He still felt no pain in his stomach. He had an enormous desire to know what had happened. The Governor came on to announce that although there had been a disaster of major proportions in Jefferson, there was no cause for panic.

The incredible stupidity of it was too much. Nerves were raw. He raged at the Governor. Another highway patrolman. A videotape of travel in Mexico. The day was darkening. A wind picked up: he could smell rain. He looked toward the silent airfield. Would like to fly again. He felt the first sense of great loss. Never to fly again. The doors were all closing. But a coldness was in his brain: *you're* not dying. He looked at his watch: ten o'clock. Rachel died in an hour. I've lived a long time.

He pieced the news together. A doctor said sternly that panic was unnecessary, that there was no sickness. Nick Tesla sat by the set and chuckled and hugged his knees. More videotapes. They seemed reluctant to give the news. Trying to avoid panic. Of course. A bit late, but it was truly incredible to sit in a world where all but you were dead and to watch television, a quiz program, a man trying to give away a refrigerator. Once again he thought: *I'm mad.*

He began to feel sleepy. He had accepted death, but now he did not think it was coming. But if it did come he would not want it to catch him sleeping. He left the set on, dragging it to the door where he could see it, staring down over the lake. He turned down the sound so that he could hear the silence. There was no wind, but there was the sound of birds. He saw a lone buzzard wheel in the sky. He thought: *you'll* be occupied. Glad I took her inside. Is that why I did it? Yes. Unconscious at work.

It should be a long day.

But it was curious, very curious, how comfortable he was. There was something about the silence that spoke to him. He felt the beginning of a great rest, relaxing. He did not mind an empty world. He looked up at the wall, remembering: a small wood plaque he'd picked up at an airport out west, in the Rockies, message from an anonymous cowboy:

> *Sweet clean air from east to west*
> *And room to go and come*
> *I loved my fellow man best*
> *When he was scattered some.*

The irony of that now, like most everything else, was unbelievable. He half slept, closing his eyes. Then he heard a patter, like small steps coming toward him. He jerked awake. But it was only the rain. He watched it come down, obscuring the lake. He thought: good thing I flew in early this morning; would've had trouble in the rain.

A foolish thought. *Trouble.* He smiled at himself. But he did not feel bad at all. He began to wonder how long it would take. And what would he do if he did not die?

Fly out of here.

No. I don't want to be sick on the plane. Don't want to die falling. Not that way. But you won't be sick. If you're going to die, how long do you wait?

The news at noon was a capsule. The area of death was an almost perfect circle around the town of Jefferson. Authorities still did not know the cause of the disaster, but latest information would indicate there was no plague; repeat: no plague. The health department had treated persons who passed through the area and died, and those people seemed to have died of radiation poisoning. There was, therefore, no reason to be alarmed unless you had been in that area. Radiation not contagious.

Nick Tesla sat in his island of silence. He thought: but no one is immune to radiation. But I am still alive. Therefore they are lying. Or the world's gone mad. Or I've gone mad.

But if it is radiation? That current I felt?

And still feel.

It was there, still there, an almost undetectable warmth. He had grown used to it, he had to probe for it, but it was there, and then he was not sure: it was only something he had imagined, or it had been there so long his nerves were used to it and bathed in it and lulled by it.

The newsman reported that the morning Eastern flight had come into Albany from Jefferson and landed. But all the passengers were taken ill, and they had all died.

Nick Tesla thought: *but they didn't even land.*

He gave up trying to understand it. He was tired. He dozed, and the rain went on falling, and then in the late afternoon it began to clear, and suddenly it was very warm. The young man sat on the steps of his house, and finally there was too much silence.

He began to walk around the house. The sky was clearing, the sun broke through; patches of brilliant blue, of clean washed air, patterned the sky. He waited but he did not get sick. He began to feel very strange—light-headed, glass-fragile brain.

There came a wind, a new breeze behind the departing storm, and he sensed the air coming up from town, something in the wind. He sniffed and waited and then he knew. In the town there had been seventy thousand people. They had been dead for many hours.

He did not want the smell. The smell of death was too much. He made up his mind. He got in the car and drove back to the airport and gassed his plane. He did not look into the office where Rachel lay. He was extraordinarily tired. He wanted out. He started up and taxied out past the rows of motionless planes, that odor beginning to fill the air, not bad yet, not truly bad, but a certain peculiar sweetness, an eerie weight, as if the air was turning heavier. He moved into position on the runway, automatically searching for other aircraft, laughed at himself. He wondered what happened to the Air Force boys in the three jets. He knew they were dead. And I'm still alive. *I'm chosen.*

He took off and climbed high up, very high, away from the silent town, the invisible dead. He flew through the beautiful air in the ancient but beautiful airplane, and then below he saw cars moving, people again, and the new motion was a new life beginning. He called ahead to the Albany tower and told them who he was and where he'd come from and when he landed there was a white truck waiting for him and men dressed all in white with plastic masks and plastic gloves, and they took him away.

TWO

General Armitage said, "It begins here."

They stopped in a grove of dark thick pines. There was a metal bar across the road, flanked by armed soldiers. They got out of the car into hot air, a musky smell. Richard Ring saw one armored car, many trucks, flocks of soldiers, a slash out through the woods where they'd built a wood fence on both sides of the road, leading into the woods away from the metal bar. An officer came forward crisply, saluted Armitage. Ring was not in uniform. He went to the metal gate, put his hands on hot iron, looked up the empty road.

It was black asphalt, rolling up through the shade of the pines to a low rise. Far to the left the pines ended and there was a sunlit field, and in the field far away there were many cows. Ring sniffed: sour mucky smell.

Armitage said, "It begins right up there"—he pointed, squinted—"about half a mile."

"How do you know where it starts?"

"Well, dammit." Armitage grunted, spread his palms, waved vaguely. "You can feel the damn thing."

Feel it? Ring looked at the thin face. Competent man. Stubborn, bright-eyed, bright red hair rather thin now like fine red wire. Ring said, "*Feel* it?"

"Yep. What the hell. I can't describe . . . listen, nobody can. But we've got the gadgetry out there, all of it, and none of it's consistent, radioactivity comes and goes like some damned wind, and nothing makes any sense, we're waiting for that Team of ours, Corelli, all those guys, but man, listen, you can *feel* the damned thing. I felt it myself. Hell of a shock. I walked in there a way and felt it and I thought it was just mental but it's damned clear and after a minute I knew it was no fluke and so I got the hell out."

Ring gazed at the thin face. He said slowly, "You seem all right. How do you feel?"

"Fine. I don't think . . . well, what the hell. It takes awhile to kill you. If you stay there long enough, it damned sure will."

"How long?"

"We had one helicopter team go off course and into the Zone. We call it the, ah, Zone. Well, they were in there about twenty minutes. Inside the Zone. They came out sick and they all died within an hour. So. I grounded the rest. If the wind gets touchy . . ."

"The wind. What about that? I mean, does the thing move?"

"Nope. Thank God. It seems to be pretty damned firm. It stays there. Up the road."

Ring whistled. Armitage nodded. He said, "Damn right," nodding his head. Ring peered thoughtfully.

"You look okay."

Armitage grinned.

"I wasn't in there long. Not long enough."

"Um." Ring tapped the metal bar. "Open up. I think I'll walk up the road a ways."

"Now, sir, now, I wouldn't advise that."

"It didn't kill you."

"Not yet, not yet. But, sir, I must insist . . ."

Ring meditated. But he had a wave of radiant curiosity. He said, "Open the gate."

A young Lieutenant looked at Armitage. He did not know who Ring was. Armitage gestured: the gate swung smoothly, oilily up. Ring walked through and onto the open road. Armitage came behind him. He said, "I'll follow you."

"Up to you."

"This is goddamn foolish, you know."

Ring grinned, walked slowly up the road, hands in his pockets. Armitage said something about authority of command, necessity to protect personnel, set an example. He was preaching. Ring loosened his formal tie. He saw birds in the trees, heard the chatter of crows. He saw no hawks or buzzards. Ahead, the cows in the fields were feeding. He said, "What's the effect on animals?"

"Don't know. Apparently nothing much. You can stand on that hill up there and see fields full of cows and horses deep in the Zone, and they're all still alive, and nothing's happened to them, or the birds either."

"Um." Ring walked. His mouth was drying. He liked the sensation of controllable fear. His body was coming alive. He topped the rise.

The road led south into green open country, farmland. To his left there were the cows, looking this way; beyond them a stand of corn. On his right a roadway sign indicated the speed limit in black letters: 55 MPH. Far up the road to the right there was one small black farmhouse with a white barn, a long stand of corn. There was a yellow tractor in a brown field. He walked. He saw a sign on the left: a feature in Florida, a busty mermaid swimming among fat fish. There was a light wind blowing from the west, rippling weeds along the side of the road. Armitage, grunting, said, "Not much farther."

"What am I supposed to feel?"

"You won't get to that farmhouse. You see that farmhouse? That's in the Zone. You have to stop this side of that."

"Do you feel anything?"

The air was windy and warm and sweet and sour. Ring heard the sudden raw bawl of a cow. It rattled him. Armitage said sweatily, "Listen, you'll know it when you feel it. You don't feel anything yet? Good. Neither do I. But I don't know. What the hell. I think I'll stop. You want to go on, go ahead. That's your business."

Armitage stopped in the center of the road. He folded his arms across his chest. His face was wet and glittering. Ring paused for a moment. But there was a magnetic pull from the dark empty road, the road going up into the silence. Ring put a hand to his mouth. He said, "Well, I'll just be a moment."

He went up into the heated air. He heard Armitage's voice but the words meant nothing. He walked. Armitage was calling something. Ring slowed. His skin was crawling. He thought abruptly: Richard, don't be a damned fool. But he walked a little farther. Felt hot air. Walked. Saw the farmhouse ahead. Motionless. Nothing there. Walked.

What came was a fever. At first he thought it was a breath of hot air. But then he felt himself shudder. His skin rippled. It was coming over him like a flow. An electric flow. A fever. His mind said: *enough.*

He turned, began to back away, then began to trot. Then he decided, hell, might's well run, and he began to run, saw Armitage down the road, crouching, waving, then turn and begin to move back toward the gate. They both ran. Ring slowed when he could clearly see the gate. Must reenter with dignity. He could feel his heart beating with heavy thumps. He slowed to a walk. Armitage was waiting, growling, shaking his head. Ring grinned.

"See what you mean," Ring said.

Armitage was examining him.

"I hope the hell you're all right."

"Hm." Ring examined himself.

"Feels like kind of a shock, right?" Armitage said.

Ring nodded.

"That's what I felt," Armitage said, cocking his head to

26

one side. "That's what most people say." Ring stopped inside the open gate, looked back up the black road. He said, "It goes on for fifty miles."

"Yep."

"In what seems to be an exact circle."

"Right."

"You've determined the center of the circle?"

"The town of Jefferson."

"Jefferson." Ring shook his head. Fifty miles. All dead. The enormity of the thing was beginning to flow in his brain. He said slowly, "Fifty miles. All dead."

Armitage said, "Some people lived through it."

"I heard that." Ring stared. "How many?"

"Very few. Dozen or so. First we thought it was a plague and they were immune . . . Christ, you should have seen this place near here when we came in and the plague rumor was out. Whee. Had to bring in my boys."

"Well, it's not plague. No bug."

"Nope. You felt it. What do you think?"

Ring shook his head.

Armitage said, "My medical boys are working. But they're pretty sure it's no germ, no plague. Certainly doesn't seem contagious. What it really looks like is radiation. But even that, dammit, the thing just doesn't register correctly on any meter—well, hell, your boys will have to look at that. Makes no sense, no sense at all, once you feel the damn thing."

"It all centers on the town of Jefferson?"

"Yep."

"What is there in Jefferson?"

Armitage sighed. "A papermill. A phosphate mine."

They moved through the gate: it closed behind them. Soldiers had flocked to watch them. Ring recognized the shoulder patch. An airborne unit he had once commanded. Will any remember me? No matter. He walked toward the staff car. He took off his tie. He was soaked through with sweat: hadn't noticed it. He said, "Turn the damned air conditioner on, John."

They drove off through deserted farm country. The people near the Zone had gone; it was miles now to the nearest crowd. He passed a deserted gas station, ancient pumps giving him a sudden memory of a late-night horror movie. He had a thought. "John, we're going to have to be prepared for movement."

"Sir?"

"The Zone could widen."

But the magnitude of the thing was too great. It was taking awhile. He sat back in the dark seat and let the cool air flow over him, relaxed; let the brain work. He was riding toward a meeting with the Team. Too soon for opinions. But he began to make notes.

At ten that morning he had been at a desk in New Jersey. He had been examining overflight photos of a peculiar construction in western China, in Sinkiang Province. It had been his job, until ten that morning, to find out what that construction was about. He had been called by Dick Hiller, orders from the President, placed in charge of the Operation, which as yet had no name, given the bare details. His jet had been on the ground at Albany, Georgia, just after noon. The rest of his Team, picked by Hiller, would arrive that night. The amazing thing was that nobody anywhere had a contingency plan for this sort of thing. Hiller was making it up as he went along, by phone from Washington. Ring smiled nastily. One stumble after another. He had seen it all his life: that stunning incompetence. Never quite got used to it. No time to think on it now. He pictured Jefferson, the dead town of Jefferson. One great mistake there. Possibly biggest mistake of all. Finally.

Ring was tall and slim and very dark, black-eyed, sharp-nosed, face so delicate it was somewhat feminine. All his life he had been very good at whatever he did. He had begun as a superb athlete; that, along with the pretty face, had delayed his maturity for a long while. He had distinguished himself in the Army, in Special Forces, a truly inspired combat officer, had risen rapidly to rank of Colonel. But he had also suddenly learned to read books for the joy of it, and he had an inquiring mind. When he was about thirty he began to grow up. He developed a great dislike, not for combat, but for the military mind. War was fun. He was becoming a bitter man with no fear of death. He did not marry. Women were easy; he had never found one he really needed. There came an opportunity to fly a mission in to South America for the CIA; he took it: it was charming. He was past forty, too late for the desk. He had no gift for diplomacy; he did not think much of mankind. He remained on leave from the Army, working through dull assignments for the CIA, and then he was shifted to a branch called Special Diplomatic Services, which was technically under the State Department and theoretically involved with the protection of diplomats and diplomatic offices around the world. The office actually did try to protect diplomats, with moderate success, but Ring's section was a collection of competent people who were available to the President for high-priority troubleshooting, a cut above normal espionage. In this job Ring learned a great deal, traveled a great deal, and eventually got to know the President, who looked at him and immediately trusted him, actually picked him out of a group one day to rely on for advice, searching out—Ring thought—almost indiscriminately, almost desperately, a groping man badly in need of advice, of people he could trust in the bureaucratic ranks below him. He fixed himself on Ring instinctively, and from then on Ring was an important man in government, although very few people knew it. He was still technically assigned to the Army, and his rank was still that of a Colonel, and his pretty face fitted in nicely with his theoretical job as a defender of diplomats. When this trouble had broken, the President had called for Ring, although the official appointment had gone to Hiller, who would be down later in the week. And so Ring had come down. He was responsible directly to the President. He did not particularly like the man. He was sorry for him but he had little respect for him: the man should never have taken the job. Ring had no great faith in the country either: the more he saw of the world, the more he concluded that nationalism was already dead. And although he moved in highly patriotic circles and heard many emotional speeches, he was untouched. He could feel the whole thing dying, the whole vast flabby edifice collapsing slowly, almost invisibly, like the falling in slow motion of a detonated cliff. Ring knew all that—the way of life was dying—something strange and dark was coming. But it was a vacant universe, a cooling world. Ring had never quite forgiven religion its failure, but now he did not much care for the future, the cold future, did not much care for anything; he did not even, at that time, have a girl anywhere, or a need of one. He had the job solely for fun, for the excitement, for the sheer curiosity. What the hell could *do* a thing like that—kill all those people? He had ideas. Could not talk about anything yet. He had already wondered if there was a possible link between this thing here and the Chinese buildings. Excitement renewed him, like a fountain of youth. His mind bubbled.

*   *   *

The scientific Team—for which the code name was temporarily "The Fus" after Dr. Fu—had arrived some hours ago and was located in a courthouse building in a small town, which had been evacuated. The leader of the Team was a small Italian named Corelli—Aldo Corelli, a bald little man with a small round white nose, somewhat like a Ping-Pong ball. Ring had met him once for a few days a few years ago examining an unexploded bomb the IRA had left in

London, but Ring did not know the little man, did not even know exactly what type of doctor he was, although he knew enough to know that Corelli was very well educated scientifically, in several different fields, and seemed to be one of those curious but not creative men who wander from field to field, probing. He was standing in a judges' private chamber when Ring came upon him, led by Armitage. Corelli had drawn a large map on paper already carefully arranged on the judges' wall, and was drawing a radius line as Ring entered.

"*Was macht* Du Villy? Ha?" Corelli giggled. He was evidently very nervous. "Ziss one hell of a mess, ha? *Nein?*" He put out a hand. "I remember you. Ring. Ole chap. London. That fella? Ya. Well, listen. Do you know *anything* about this?" He gloomed, searching Ring's face, then shrugged to Armitage. "They never tell you, these fellas. Hell, he could know it all, the whole goddamn schmear, but he wouldn't . . ."

"Hell, you know why." Ring was gazing at the map. A town in the center, a circle around it. Dotted lines. Jefferson. A small university.

"Why? Because this one, listen, this one . . ."

"Because if anybody from across the pond ever picks me up for questioning, or you, or any of us, the less we know the better. Right? So don't bother to ask any questions. Just the facts. What happened?"

"Ah." Corelli grunted. He crossed himself. "I don't know how . . . well, all right. One by one." He took a breath, plucked a cigarette from an inside pocket, lighted, squinted at the map, picked up a long baton pointer.

"The beginning," Corelli said. He paused. "First report was at, ah, to be exact"—he peered at some small numbers he had written on the side of the map—"at 2:24 A.M. Hospital call from a truckstop located here." He pointed to a black X marked on a road leading roughly out of the town

31

drawn on the map, just outside the dotted line that circled the town. "Some truckers got sick and threw up and the waitress called for an ambulance because one looked dead. And he was. And then, in the ambulance, the other died on the way in. That's where it started. Few minutes later the same thing happened over here." He pointed east of town, to another black X. "This time only one driver. He went into the bathroom and died there. Then, right here, there was a car crash. Exact time unknown, but pretty close to 2:30 A.M. Fella went off the road with his whole family in the car—four people—hit a tree. Highway patrolman saw the flame, drove over there, they were all dead, no apparent reason—then a little while later, 3:04—the patrolman called back and said he was sick. Didn't call again. Has not come out. Is still in there, presumed dead. Then there were more reports from that same truckstop, same thing, and then, well, they began to spread. One call came from a highway patrolman, all alone in the dark, very fuzzy, that he felt lousy. Then from him: nothing. Then a muffled call from a Sheriff's deputy, asking help for a problem we can't decipher. Again, nothing more. No answer. Not even to phone calls, which began to start about this time to the police stations. That's about it. A few more people came driving out of that town very sick, pulled off the road, and died at the side of the road, in a few moments, and some pulled into a gas station or restaurant and died there. The Highway Patrol—that's what they call it here, not State Police—couldn't raise anybody inside that area. They sent two guys in at . . . 4:00 A.M."

Corelli stopped, ran up the map with his finger along a southern road. "Both drove down empty roads for about twenty minutes, saw nothing moving anywhere; then, after about twenty minutes, they called back that they were sick. Then—no more. They're still there. So at 4:30 the Sheriff here called the Governor's office. Somebody at the Governor's office called you. From then on it began to break. The word of the dead, I mean, because nobody else came out of that place, and we apparently had begun to learn enough to stay the hell out. Because if you went inside past about here"—he pointed at the point on the map where the road touched the wide dotted circle—"you got sick, and pretty soon died. Takes about—twenty minutes. One of the first things the police did wrong at daybreak was to fly a chopper in over the area. Men wore gas masks. Yes. Gas masks. All they did was get this far, about twenty miles in, and they quieted down. They put the chopper down in a field, and they're still there. Then just after the dawn came the big thing. An Eastern jet, which was scheduled to land at Jefferson, didn't—it circled and then came up to Albany and landed. Just barely got down, because they were all sick. Everybody. Crew and everybody. Nobody well enough to walk off the plane. All dead within a few minutes. All. Well, that sort of . . . started the fan."

Ring took a deep breath, blew a silent whistle.

"Yep." Corelli nodded.

"What is it?" Ring said.

"Glad you asked me that." Corelli blinked, plucked his nose.

Ring waited.

"Well," Corelli gloomed. "Well, it's radiation."

"Radiation."

"Yep."

"Radiation?"

"Yep. Only."

"Only what?"

"It's . . . I can't describe it. That's why I want to know . . . hell, you know how things can be made radioactive, almost anything, and *you* know, if anyone does, the work that went into putting out the neutron bomb. But this . . . isn't normal radiation. Not quite. It moves . . . it doesn't move in a straight line."

"A straight line."

"What I mean . . . hell, I don't know what I mean. But I'll describe it. Right there, in the center of that town, is a source of massive radiation. Something that sprays. And when I say massive, buddy, I mean *massive*. It comes about here"—he indicated the exact center of his dotted circle, the heart of the town—"which means it's located in or near that little university, which is damned interesting. But what the thing is, is . . . a kind of . . . *fountain*. It just sprays in all directions, these tiny particles which are God knows what, and the wind doesn't seem to affect them. It's not exactly . . . well, it's brand new. It's a particle that's blowing like hell through everything in a rather odd way, yet seems to follow gravity. I think it's a particle with a new . . . field. It touches some things, but others . . . show no trace. It seems to be sailing right through most things, most living objects. But not people. People it hits harder than . . . normal radiation. And yet it seems to do no harm to anything else. Fellas on the chopper reported cows and horses moving. I saw birds fly in and out myself. Now what . . . a damned fountain. Right there. At the University."

Moment of silence. Ring put his fingers over his eyes. Had thought of gas, a wrecked train, germ warfare. But not . . . The Fountain. In a moment he was relieved. Then he remembered the Chinese action. The Chang Po Effect.

Ring said, "A fountain?"

Corelli edged the finger around the map.

Ring said, "And it doesn't move? Wind doesn't affect it?"

"There's not been much wind. But . . . it seems to puff out in a fountain shape, rising and falling. Just along this road here—here, you can detect almost nothing—and then a few yards farther down it is suddenly massive and lethal, and you can feel it, although you certainly see nothing, and birds fly right by . . ."

Ring said, "The University."

"Check."

"Do you know anything? Any guesses?"

"Not a bean. Not a clue."

"Does it do any research involving radiation?"

"Don't know. Listen, I . . . it's a very small, ah, state-run school. A quiet place."

"Well, okay. Start that moving. You know what to do. But do you think that possibly . . . hell."

"What do I think?"

"Was it an accident?"

Corelli put a hand to his mouth.

"Ah."

"Or. Was it done on purpose?"

Corelli said nothing, stared at the wall.

Ring asked, "Can it be turned off? The source . . . in there?"

"That . . . is at least possible. But . . ."

"You think *we* can turn it off?"

"Maybe. Yes. If . . ."

"Suppose a big wind comes up. Like a hurricane. Will it blow that stuff, that *lethal* stuff?"

"I don't know. Look, I just don't know. I'm not Fu Manchu, damn it. Give me some time."

"Okay. Sorry. Well, get the teams moving. Everything you can find out about that school—Jefferson—and the people in it, what they were doing, but also the businesses in that town, whatever kind of business that has even a remote connection, find out all of it, fast as possible. And General, you and I will be bringing in some equipment that can go into a radioactive zone. Ah . . . what?"

"Just one thing." Armitage was blinking widely, rubbing his red hair. He had a dazed look in his eyes, as if he was embarrassed by what he had to say, as if some of his troops had done something truly degrading, beyond his help, but his fault and no other's. "Sir. One other thing."

"What?"

"Some people came out of there . . . alive. And . . . they're still alive now. I think you should see . . ."

Ring turned, stared at him. Corelli gave a vague smile and shook his head. Armitage raised both hands, palms up.

"All right, I'll tell you. Then you go see. In the late afternoon a young pilot flew out of that town, Jefferson, flew out of it after having been there all day—he claimed—since sunup. He flew out and landed at Albany because he said he wanted to get away from the dead. We put him under close arrest, of course, and isolated him, under observation, and found absolutely nothing wrong. So. He couldn't have been in Jefferson that day all that day. Eight hours. Impossible. Or just a fluke. But there's more."

Armitage held up two wide-parted fingers.

"There have been several more. I would not have told you if . . . that was not true. I don't yet know how many. But the next I heard of was one man who . . . who drove his car out of that lethal Zone with his family inside getting sicker every minute, and when he finally came to a stop at that truckstop there, outside the town, they all died. But he didn't. We put him in an ambulance and brought him in like the other fella, the pilot, and isolated him, and he's near here under sedation now. And . . . he has no symptom of anything . . . sick. Nothing. And then there was another like that over here, that I haven't seen but I heard about. A woman. At Cross's Point. Her friend in the car: dead. Her: perfectly normal. And then there was one man on a busload. One man lived and all the rest died, and the one man shows *no aftereffects whatsoever.* And there are a few more came driving out of that town alone, early in the morning, alone in their own cars, half gone out of their minds, because they'd wakened to find their families dead. Everybody dead. Everybody. I saw one. She was a small elderly lady, at least seventy. Slept there all night, breathed all night, and didn't die. Not particularly healthy. But . . . there are more. We have them all isolated. I want you to take a look, sir, as soon as . . ."

"People were in there . . . how long?" Ring asked.

Armitage said, "Hours. No less than six to eight hours. In a town where it takes . . . about twenty minutes to get you."

"Absolutely sure?"

"God knows."

Corelli looked at Ring. He said, "Pig 311."

Armitage said, "What?"

Corelli said, "There was a pig at an atoll once that lived right through an A-bomb blast when all the rest died, and nobody could figure out why. They thought he was a fluke. But . . . immune? Was it possible to be . . . Christ in Heaven."

"How many are you holding?" Ring asked Armitage.

"Eighteen."

Ring blew a breath. "What was the population of that town?"

"About seventy thousand."

"Seventy thousand dead. Any . . . communication with anyone in there, still in there?"

"The town seems stone dead. Nothing comes out now. Or goes in. No radio or TV. Nothing. Except those very few people. Well, there may be more inside."

Ring said, "Jesus."

Long moment of silence. Ring looked at Corelli.

"Listen. Are you telling me some people are *immune*? To radiation?" Corelli stood blinking. He said slowly, amazement in his wide eyes, "That's . . . what appears to be . . ."

Armitage said, "Must be just a fluke. Must be."

Corelli blinked again, shook his head. "No. It's possible. I don't know quite how. But I know . . . all I know . . . some people have what seems to be a high resistance. I know that. There's been some research, but as far as I know . . . it came up with nothing. They thought at first it was just plain luck. But no two people are alike. Some people . . . I knew a man once come back with a bullet in his brain, and he's alive now, and doing fine. I've heard stories . . . that the more radiation comes, the more likely it is that people will adapt to it, if there's time. Maybe there's been . . . enough time."

Ring whistled. "For who?"

Corelli said, "You have to ask God."

Armitage said, "I can't . . . believe that . . ."

Corelli put out a warning hand. "Tell you this. They went to work on the neutron bomb, and I know something about that. The idea was to produce radiation without the bomb, the big blast, and radiation that was in control, would not stay radioactive indefinitely. And that they did. Some friends . . . well, the other thing they wanted, and Ring, *you* must know this, they wanted radiation from something other than uranium, plutonium, if possible. And I think they got it. Check it out. *You* can. Hell, even I know that can be done. Look at radiation therapy. But there's something about the radiation coming out of Jefferson—something like a kind of . . . *charge.* Yes. How else do you describe it? Not positive, negative, maybe even, hell I don't know. Maybe it just . . . bounces off some people."

"How many?"

"I don't know."

"But there are . . . seventy thousand dead."

"Yes."

"So. Could be just . . . a fluke."

Corelli cocked his head. "I don't . . . think so."

"Um."

Armitage said, "I always figured sooner or later some crazy bastard was going to get hold of an A-bomb, hell, just twenty pounds . . ."

Ring said, "The guy in the airplane. You say he flew out of there, after being in town all day."

"Yep."

"He said . . . what did he say?"

"You talk to him. He didn't see anybody. He left . . . expected to die, and didn't, and then decided to leave. He sounded . . . genuine."

"How old is he?"

"Ah. About . . . twenty-eight. I think."

"I want to see him."

"Right."

Armitage said, "Immunity? I don't believe . . . radiation . . . is a million bullets. You can't . . ."

Corelli said, "More than a million. Much more. But you know . . . whatever you don't expect . . . is always the way things seem to end."

Ring said to Corelli, "All you can get out of research that was being done in that town, by anybody from anywhere, hop to it. You have A-Prime, Dr. Fu. Armitage, don't talk about immunity, to anybody. Don't leak out information . . . hell, keep it cool. Just let it slip that it was probably a gas leak, but it's controlled now, or . . . well, you know, people are familiar with that kind of gassy wreck, and there's been a lot of it, so it'll calm things a bit, long as you say the main problem is all over, long over. Just stay away from the town, station the troops, you know the rest. Nobody goes in. Catch anybody or anything that comes out that can be caught. And not a word about radiation. Clear? Fine. Now . . . before I go see this guy who says he was in there eight hours, the one who flew out, I want him checked out all the way, and everybody else who came out of that town, the old lady, etcetera. All the way. So I know as much as possible about what they have, what may strike, in what direction we'll have to move. And we're going to have to move, gentlemen, as never before. So. I want those tanks from Texas. Armitage, you know the ones I mean. For radiation. Right. Now, I'll get on the wire to Washington, and *everything* you do is A-Prime, and send on the word."

He was moving toward the door, which had been closed behind him to keep tight security, as was done in all places by Armitage's airborne troops, and Ring opened the door, saw two very big soldiers, helmeted, ready, and turned with a cheery grin.

"Hell of a job. Don't you love this stuff, Dr. Fu?"

"Um. Long as we don't run into Strangelove."

* * *

Nick Tesla alone in a pale green room. People in masks and robes and helmets came and went, for four days, testing him, asking questions, but there was no one to talk to. There were nurses sometimes behind the masks, but their hair was tucked away and even their legs were covered and there was no way to tell what anyone looked like. It was entertaining, and eerie, and he did not really mind being alone, except for the lack of women. There was no window in the room. There was a large glass mirror, and he did not know until after the first few days that they could see him through the mirror but he could not look back. The only way he knew that was because they began to ask questions about things he had been doing when no one was there, and that annoyed him. They were looking at him, even in the damned dark. He did not mind being seen naked, but he minded not being alone. On the fourth day he began to rumble.

Nick Tesla was a large man. He had big round shoulders and a damaged face, and to most men he resembled a football player: a lineman. He talked with natural intensity, moving his big thick hands in the air around him: he did not often argue. He had lived alone since the death of his parents, killed in a car wreck when he was eighteen. He had never healed the loneliness of that. He had never found another home. He had one older brother he had not seen in years and a family of aunts and uncles, most of whose children he had never met. He had quit college after the death of his parents and gone flying, and eventually got a job as a commercial pilot flying equipment—military, often illegal—overseas. He had flown the guns everywhere, seen much death, crashed three times. The last time he went down in the Arabian Desert and survived, sitting among the dead for three days watching the great stars, waiting for the death that did not come: a kind of religion was born in him. He began talking, alone at night, to the God who wasn't there. There was no answer. He was picked up by what had to be luck and sent back to the States to recover. He didn't go to church, but he began to go on talking to a silent God. He didn't believe in Jesus or even Moses or any of the command- ments, and there was never any voice anywhere, never any rules, and yet he had searched all his life for a pattern, a system, a reason beyond all of it, and he had no message as to what the rules were, but he knew they were there. Sometimes he disapproved. He scolded an absent God about the pain that was left here behind, all that suffering. He sometimes thought that the Thing that undoubtedly lived way out there was truly terrible: a genuine Devil.

But he always came back to the beauty of the earth, the midnight splendor, the grace of the women. He had begun to conclude that he was alive here on earth to do something perhaps dangerous, perhaps through a necessary pain, but he did not yet know what, was not yet sure of anything at all, could not even talk about it to anyone else he knew anywhere, except sometimes in the black nights to the God who wasn't there. And now the God—or Devil—had killed the town. And left him alive. He sat in the hospital waiting again for some word, some explanation to be given sometime by someone, but nothing came. Part of his mind knew

41

absolutely that nothing ever would, but he went on waiting anyway, in permanent hope. He waited alone, in an empty room.

He took that for four days. When he learned that they were watching him, always watching him, that the mirror was Big Brother, he felt the birth of a possibly serious rage. He withdrew. On the morning of the fourth day he refused any further tests or discussions and told a small man to get the hell out of the room. The man departed. Nick was left alone for a long while, but he was not alone and he knew it. He knew they were watching him through that damned mirror. He backed off within himself. He fell asleep.

He had a wild white dream.

It came like a vision, like an eerie movie seen at a distance, but taken by a marvelous camera with a superb lens. There was a long green slope, waves of pale green grass, green like the wall of his room but unique because he was not used to color in his dreams, his dream had little color, and the remarkable thing was that he knew all along he was dreaming, gazing at a long green slope with light hairy green grass blowing in the wind on a sunny day, and then there were poppies in the grass, bright red spots like poppies, like a painting of Renoir, and then over the crest of the hill, down the slope through the blowing grass came a couple, a boy and a girl hand in hand, the girl lovely, *lovely* blonde and blue-eyed, wide-eyed, breasts bobbing in a white blouse, *running* down, legs long and white under a pale skirt, and the two came hand in hand quickly down the long green slope but the boy had no face to recognize, nothing to see mainly because Nick didn't look at his face, the girl was too lovely, and the long legs coming out from under the pink skirt stirred his stomach, he rumbled inside, and then he saw the dead bodies: ribs, white ribs, of bodies, and a row of separate skulls, clean white bones, half buried in the grass. The couple ran by. Nick saw one large eyeless skull. Then in the grass to the right there was another set of bones, one rising knee, another skull, with the black holes of eyes, and the grass went on blowing but the skulls were motionless, and the couple was happy and giggling and did not notice the bodies as they passed, the boy patting the girl on the butt as they passed another corpse, and the girl, very young, giggling, not looking, and then down past the skeletons at the bottom of the slope there was water: bright water. The edge of a river. They stopped and knelt by the water and put down their hands to wash their faces. And here and there all up the long slope were fragments of white bones, but they were very mild and pleasant to see, almost like a new set of flowers, nothing at all disturbing, and the girl down by the river had a loose white blouse and it was down lower over her shoulder and she had fine, fine breasts, and Nick awoke.

The dream stayed there, like an eerie vision. Like a movie he'd just seen. He usually didn't remember dreams. But this one, if he closed his eyes he could see the white bones, the faces, the slope of quiet death. But he felt nothing, certainly no fear. All he felt was sex for the girl.

To himself he said, "Nick, you're a weirdo. Why dream a thing like that?"

He began to awake to the memory of the dead town. He began to feel rather strange. Suddenly, and rather strongly, he wanted out of that hospital. He wanted back in to real life. He got out of bed, went looking for his clothes. None there. He began to talk to the damned mirror but he couldn't go on with that, talking to himself in an empty room. He saw: the water pitcher. He picked it up, hefted it, felt—oh, lovely, lovely—now, let's see if it'll work. He was moving toward the mirror when the door opened and a man came in, a tall thin man with a crowd behind him, but the man shut out the crowd, closed the door, stood there alone, face calm, pleasant, silvery tie, black suit. The man gave a formal nod. A confident man. Careful eyes. Government? Nick said, tapping the pitcher, "You the boss man?"

The man smiled slightly. He nodded. "My name is Ring. I'm in charge. Mind if I sit down?"

Nick pointed. Ring moved to the chair by the TV set, took out cigarettes.

"You mind?"

"No."

"Filthy habit." Ring sat, lighted a cigarette. A neat and tidy man. Expensive clothes. Nick said, "Have you been watching me through that goddamn mirror?"

Ring nodded. "Sorry."

"I've had it," Nick said. He opened his mouth to give out the rules, but something stopped him. No longer rage: sudden enormous curiosity. "All right. If anybody knows, you do. What happened?"

Ring went on smiling the business smile. "I don't know. That's why I'm here," he said.

"What? Why?"

"You look fine, son. Nothing wrong at all. Everyone says you're fine. Isn't that amazing?"

Ring puffed, cocked his head to one side. "Mr. Tesla, I'll get to the point. I don't know what happened. I don't know why you're still alive. Nobody knows why you're still so healthy. Untouched. No aftereffects. None at all. It's . . . three things." Ring held up three fingers. "One, you're a freak. An incredible accident. All the little bullets went right on through and somehow missed you. Impossible odds. But there you are. But . . . I don't think that's it. Two." Ring tapped the second finger. "You have a natural resistance that's built in. You have . . . a remarkable constitution. You're the kind that takes a long time to die. Now, what does that mean? Who the hell knows? You lived through eight hours in there. You might last another day, another week, or"—Ring tapped the third finger—"three. You're totally immune. Radiation can't hurt you. Your body is . . . has . . . negative charge. That's possible, but I don't believe that either. Question is, if you went back in there, how long would you last?"

Nick sat on the bed. Ring watched him. He said, "That's what I came to talk about."

Nick put down the pitcher. After a moment Nick said, "How many other people came out?"

"A few."

"How many?"

Ring watched him calmly, thoughtfully, then said, "Eighteen."

Nick took a deep breath.

"Eighteen?"

"Yes."

"Jesus!" Nick said. He blinked. Remembered the young black boy running in the vacant morning. World of . . . seventy thousand dead. Nick said, "Why me?"

"Ah." Ring puffed. "That's what we'd like to find out."

Nick looked at the mirror. World of the absent God. Ring said cheerily, "You can help. If you want to."

"Eighteen."

"Have something to ask you."

"I'd like to meet some of them."

"Oh, fine. But. Going to ask you a favor."

Nick turned back, stared through a puff of smoke. Ring said, "You're clearly healthy. Nothing at all wrong. May just be luck, but . . . *but*"—Ring chuckled, shook his head —"hell, I'll get to the point. Are you willing to go back into the town?"

The man stood up, put his hands in his pockets.

"Dangerous? Hell, yes. But I don't think so. Not for you. Of course I could be wrong, and if I'm wrong, you'll die. Yep. Hell of a gamble. But . . . we need you. I think myself that

45

it's worth it. We want to know what's in there. We want to know where the thing is coming from and why it's still working and who did it and how, *but* . . ."—he pointed one long slim finger at Nick—"we have no other way to get in. None at all. No usable shield. We can't even fly in close enough to do what's necessary. All we can do is bomb the town, if necessary, but we don't even know exactly where it is, so if we do that we blow the whole thing to hell and gone. *But* . . . you lived there for eight hours. Almost ten hours. No aftereffect at all. So. We think you'd make it. You'll find something in there. The, ah, weapon. Take you one or more hours. Maybe two. We all think you'll make it. But we could all be wrong. Well, what do you think?"

Nick stared at the man, looked back at the mirror, at himself.

Ring said, "Take your time. If we thought it was really bad, we might ask you anyway. I don't know. But . . . well, you know that. You know how . . . politicians will talk. But. Think on it. One thing more. This is a formal request. From the President."

Nick grunted.

They sat for a long moment in silence. Nick thought: empty road. Into a dead town. Rachel's body . . . five days dead. World gone mad. Absent God. Nick said, "What do you want? Exactly?"

"Ah. Well, we put you in a car and you drive on in. We give you some, ah, equipment. You drive in close and use it. Find the, ah, *source*. If possible, you may even be able to turn the thing off. Well. You keep in touch all the way. It'll take you . . . two hours. Maybe a little more."

"Um."

"Two hours."

Nick whistled. Ring grinned. "Hell of a gamble," Ring said.

Nick said, "Seventy thousand dead."

"Yep."

"Whew!"

"But they all died at night. Almost all. In bed. Inside the houses. You know that. You saw very few. You won't see many. That's one gift."

"What about the smell?"

"Ah." Ring raised both hands. "Should be terrible, right? Dead five days. But it isn't. Smell almost undetectable. Makes no sense, but there it is. Truth. Smell is no problem. Maybe because of the manner of death. But . . . you've seen a few dead already. I know that. I've . . . looked in to your record. The dead you've seen were a lot worse than what you'll see here. But, well, how about that? Will all the dead stop you?"

Nick put a hand to his mouth, rubbed his cheek. He said, "I don't think so."

Ring nodded. "I didn't think so either. One reason I've come to you. You've seen violent places. As I have."

Nick thought: studying me. Military mind? Nick said slowly, "I could fly in."

"Thought of that. Rather you don't. Drive. Safer that way. And we'll give you equipment in a car you can have with you at all times. Take a little longer, sure, but we'd rather you drive in."

"Um."

"When this is over, you should ask for an airplane." Ring grinned, watching. "Replace your Stinson with something new. They'll . . . owe it to you."

Nick leaned forward, rested his chin on his hand. Ring lighted another cigarette. After a silent moment Ring said, "Mind if I ask you a personal question? No? Your . . . occupation was that of a commercial pilot, for an, ah, private party overseas. Across the pond. Is that correct?"

"Yep."

"I gather you flew a lot of interesting equipment into

47

interesting places at night. Ireland. Rhodesia. Places like that."

Nick glanced at Ring's face, then away. Ring said cheerily, "Like to talk about that, if there's time. Off the record, of course. But. I gather you don't belong to anybody."

"Belong?"

"I mean, you don't join any cause. Any party. No politics. You did the flying mainly for the money. That correct?"

"No."

"No?"

"No."

"Ah. Then if you don't mind my asking, why *did* you do that stuff? Which was always rather dangerous. Why? Not for the money?"

"Not even that." Nick shrugged. No way to explain. "I . . . just like to fly. I love . . . to fly. They paid me to do it. And for a while there it was interesting, as you say."

Ring watched, waiting. Then Ring said, "What caused that last crash? In the desert. Was it gunfire?"

"No."

"What was it? I'm curious."

"Lightning."

"Um." Ring grunted. "Thunderstorm?"

"Yep."

"In the desert. Ha. Killed five men. But not you."

"Yep."

"You're a lucky fella."

"Amen."

"Well." Ring puffed. "Well, want to talk about money?"

"Money?"

"There'll be some"—Ring paused—"compensation, of course. Not much. Hell. Certainly not worth the risk. But. Just thought I'd mention it."

Nick stroked his cheek. He thought: eighteen. Ring said, "Well, any questions?"

"No."

"Well, think on it."

Ring took a step toward the door. He paused. "Take your time, son. Anything you want here? Anything for dinner? Go ahead, ask. You're a special guest." Ring smiled. "Ask for anything. Specialty of the house."

He stood there, watching. Nick said, "Come to think of it, I'd like a bottle of wine. White wine."

"White. Dry? Chablis? Any special kind?"

"Chablis is fine."

"Okay. Wilco." Ring put a hand on the doorknob. Nick said, "Two hours. That's what you want."

Ring nodded. Nick said slowly, "Strange thing. God-damn."

"Yup."

"You know, I'm curious."

Ring nodded. "Me too."

"Okay," Nick said.

Ring watched him. "Think on it," Ring said.

"I'll go. When do you want me to go?"

"Tomorrow."

"Okay. Fine."

"Think on it."

"Okay."

Ring stood there. Nick's heart took a skipping beat. Ring said, "If there's anything at all you need . . ."

Nick nodded, stood up.

"Well." Ring stood with his hand at the door. "I'll drop by later. Listen, there's no pressure."

"Oh, yes there is."

"What?"

"I'd like to know . . . why *me*. Any reason at all. Or . . . a freak."

Ring said slowly, "See what you mean." He grimaced. "But you know . . . I wish I could go."

49

"It's a dead town."

"What the hell," Ring said. He opened the door: a mass of faces, clatter of voices. "Think on it." He closed the door.

Nick sat for a long while seeing nothing. He did not look into the mirror; he stared at the floor.

Eighteen.

That night, when he lay in the dark, he did not talk to the absent God.

* * *

Ring stepped out into the green hall. They were all waiting. Corelli, the tiny Italian, grabbed his arm.

"Well, will he go?"

Ring nodded.

"He will? Oh, lovely!" Corelli was delighted. Ring blinked. He thought of Nick's face: big and bruised, calm and grinning. He thought: the boy must have already thought of it. Corelli was saying happily, "He really doesn't mind going in there, with all the dead in there?"

"He'll go tomorrow. I told him to think on it. But he'll go."

Ring freed himself from Corelli's grip. He said, to all the faces, "Time to move."

Corelli nodded.

"Right, we've got them all waiting. Listen, did you tell the kid anything about this?"

"No."

They went off together down the hall, Corelli at Ring's side, the others behind him. The others were two of Ring's aides, silent messengers, and two uniformed soldiers, messengers from Armitage. Corelli was the only one who spoke to Ring. The others dropped back. Corelli said, "Listen, one thing has come up. Finally."

"Yes?"

"Do you know A. M. Shepherd?"

"Who?"

"A. M. Shepherd. You've heard of him. Won the Nobel a few years ago."

"Shepherd?"

"The genetics nut. But he won a *Nobel*. You don't remember?"

"Why? What?"

"Well, he went into that town a few days ago. Came in from Rome, Italy. Went in on a visit to somebody. He hasn't come out, apparently."

Ring stopped, peered at Corelli's cheery face.

"What's the point?"

"I have no idea."

"Well, check it out."

"We are."

"Shepherd." Ring blinked, tried to remember. Nothing came. He saw Nick's face. Going in tomorrow. Will he live?

"Interesting," Corelli said. "Shepherd was rather a big gun. An oddball, yes, but a first-class technician and the only clue we've got so far about anything scientific, anything at all. Probably only a visit, but he's a big man to be going to a place like *that,* where there was nothing going on that we know of. He's . . . well, let it go."

"Check it out." They went on walking.

"Right. Oh, one other thing. Rather minor, but it's your problem now."

"What?"

"We've had a series of sticky requests. Sorry. A flock of residents of, ah, the town Jefferson weren't there the night the radiation started. They were out of town. A few salesmen, some lawyers, people like that. Not too many, but the requests are piling up. They want to go back in." He glanced quizzically at Ring. Ring shook his head.

Corelli said, "I told 'em they'd have to wait a bit, that we had to clean the place out and it might take us some time, but . . . well, their families, all their kids, you know . . ."

They came to the door of the main hall. Guards came to attention. The door was opened; Ring took a deep breath, calmed himself, went through the crowd and the noise and the smoke, passed familiar faces, nodded, smiled, nodded, said nothing, did not say hello. He recognized many faces but personally knew none of them. They were people from the news media who had been approved for a briefing by the President's office. Ring had to say something. They were all watching him, faces following him with eyes like cameras. He felt acutely watched, acutely cautious, controlled himself, seemed outwardly cold and calm and slightly smiling. There was Armitage at a lectern. Ring went there and stood behind the lectern facing the faces, nodding, looking, heard Armitage introduce him. All the men were sitting. There were no women. There was much smoke in the air. It was remarkably quiet. Ring took a deep breath.

"Gentlemen,"—he paused, puffed, smiled—"this is going to be rather difficult. I have no experience in this matter. But I'll tell it as best I can. This is what I've been authorized to tell you. You all know the conditions. All this is very, very touchy. Well, let me begin by saying that we have no explanation for what's been going on. None. We don't know why that town died. We don't know if it was an accident or if it was done deliberately. We don't know any of that. But, there are a few things we do know. These are all facts. I can vouch for them as facts. But what they mean"—Ring held up his hands—"listen, judge for yourself."

He stopped, waited for a moment, calmed himself, began to chat in a soft, slow, quiet, rational voice. They leaned forward to hear him.

"The first fact has been kept top secret. Here it is. On April 29, not quite two years ago, a number of soldiers on a foreign border, just above the . . . desert, a number of foreign soldiers, approximately three hundred, suddenly died."

"Suddenly." Ring paused. "In about an hour. There was no radiation. It was too quick for any known plague. It could not have been food poisoning. Within two hours their leaders were . . . upset. They were moving in on their enemies, at which time they discovered that there were also a number of dead soldiers across the border line. On the other side. How many, we have never discovered. They sat and waited. Nothing else happened. Nobody else died. Nobody has died there since then. The cause of death was never determined. Not that we know of. We never have explained it to our own satisfaction. Our only evidence indicated sudden massive radiation, but there was no evidence of any radiation, no evidence of anything radioactive. So. That was the first fact. It was kept quiet. I assume you can see why. Neither side released any information. We did not say what we knew. But we were very curious. We moved in . . . as you may know . . . in whatever ways were possible. We found nothing. The British actually suspected flying saucers." Ring smiled politely. "We gave that a thought ourselves. But we found nothing concrete. Then the next thing happened.

"Approximately two months later, in June of that year, in an area of western *China* much farther than the border area, several hundred people suddenly died. We did not find that out immediately, but within a few days. We had less evidence and, as you know, did not release it. But . . . a small town died. Almost to the man. Size approximately eight thousand." Ring paused. Nobody moved. He took his time, telling it slowly, carefully, accurately.

"We put the two together. But we found nothing to explain it. For a while we thought it could have been a radiation accident, but . . . our research did not corroborate that diagnosis." He smiled, shrugged. "Research reached no conclusion. But . . . we began to get rather nervous. So did the Soviets. The point was simply that the thing was lethal and inexplicable and quite possibly a very dangerous weapon, the worst anyone has yet come up with, and so of course we did the best we could, and so did the Soviets, but we had no evidence at all of anything. No evidence. Just death. Quiet, sudden death. Then came Fact three.

"Approximately one year ago. A year ago this month. You know of this. A series of deaths in San Francisco. In one week. Several each day. Published cause was botulism. Fish poisoning. News release covered the deaths of approximately forty-five people. The CDC went in right away. And so did we. The deaths, you see, and this is the thing I cannot explain . . . the deaths were not botulism, and the only thing we could note about them was that they resembled the deaths we'd heard of, but not seen, in the foreign country. Ah. One other item. The deaths in our own country seemed to have been caused by radioactivity. But there was no detectable radiation in that town. None at all. We moved as best we could, as quietly as possible, in to university research. We were . . . understaffed. We did . . . what we could. We tried to find *some* clue, anything at all. Chemical warfare of some kind. Germ warfare. But the deaths, as you recall, went on for only a few days and then stopped. There was no evidence of anything dangerous happening. We checked out laboratories as best we could, but it was . . . very difficult. And we found nothing. Clues here and there about possibly dangerous work, but only theoretical, no proof. Our own work on the neutron bomb . . . proved nothing. *Nothing.*"

Ring shook his head. He looked at the faces, saw open mouths.

"For several months there was nothing. Nothing at all anywhere. Not overseas that we know of. Nothing. Rather quiet time. And then, you will of course remember this, and link it, a few deaths in Seattle. Farther up the coast from San Francisco. Only about twenty known deaths. Again, the cause was stated to be botulism. But it wasn't. We moved in our experts, our few people, and they found the same sort of death, apparently due to radioactivity, which again simply wasn't there. We were investigating Seattle when the next incident occurred, in Milan, Italy. *Milan.* We were able, as you may know, to check that out. Similar death. So. There it sat. Until the town of Jefferson . . . died. Totally died."

Ring fished in his shirt, brought out a cigarette. His nerves were raw; he needed the damned thing. He heard somebody quietly swear. He nodded, in that direction.

"True. Hell of a thing. Just one more fact. About ten days ago, a small plague began in Jefferson. Cause unknown. We didn't hear about it. It was reported to the CDC in Atlanta. They went down there four days ago." He paused. "They have not come out. So, now. You see the point, gentlemen. You see the point. Not just a few. Not even a few hundred. Now, seventy thousand. And there is radioactivity detectable now, and it is very different from anything we've ever known, or can explain, and this time it not only has come on, it will not stop. So. There's where it stands. Now, any questions?"

Silence. They were not even looking at each other. They were looking at him, or at the floor. Ring said slowly, "Anything you have to say, anything, I'll welcome. We shall shortly discuss how much of this you wish to make public. But . . . all the rest I can tell you is only a theory of my own, and could be dead wrong, but here's what I think. There's some sort of *machinery* in there, in that town, that's lethal. It was invented by . . . someone . . . not too long ago, and is . . . almost certainly one of the most powerful and practical weapons ever made. It kills just . . . *people* . . . same basic design as the neutron bomb. No great heat, no blast. Just . . . radiation. But about that, this kind of radiation . . ."

Ring paused. No words came. No way to explain this. They were not expecting this. So.

"This kind of radiation is as yet . . . unknown. But it's certainly . . . different. One other thing. As you may have heard, some people in there have survived and come out. How long they'll live, no way of knowing. But . . . this radiation does not have an . . . equal effect on people. Hell, may just be a fluke. We always knew that some things survive normal radiation a lot easier than others, and this is a new type, so we just . . . don't know what it is. But, well, I'll put it this way. You may hear that some people are . . . immune. Well, I say that now only for this reason: if you've heard of any research being done anywhere by anybody that links up with this, let us know. Now. Instantly."

He looked around the room. Blank faces. No motion. Stunned. Ring nodded to himself. They didn't expect it either. Well. Soften the blow.

"Well, all we know is that some people survived, and there were some of us who were expecting that. Always possible. But, there is a source of radiation in that town that's quite possibly controllable . . . *stoppable* . . . and if it is, well, we'll stop it. If necessary. Gentlemen, we may have to hit that town. Because you see this, it's always possible, gentlemen, that the thing in there is not a mistake."

Ring paused, locked his arms behind his back.

"Not a mistake. It may only have been an experiment. Yes. But if not . . . well, we're going on in tomorrow to investigate. We have some . . . volunteers. Tomorrow should be . . . interesting. In the meantime, any information you have, anything, please pass on to my boys as soon as you can. If you've ever heard, in the lightest gossip, any word of some scientist . . . or anybody . . . who was tinkering with radiation, of any kind . . ."

Ring stopped.

"Any guesses, fellas?"

Nothing.

Ring smiled. Then he grinned, shrugged. "I tell you, boys, I hope to God . . . could this same thing happen again? Happen somewhere else? Closer to home? And if so . . . Now. Any questions?

THREE

The morning was gray. The sky was a gray roof just over the treetops and Nick knew he couldn't fly up into it and find the airport inside the Zone, but they didn't plan that anyway. Luck. He had breakfast and many pills on a gray morning watched by many quiet people, no longer masks on the faces, and he saw his own face once briefly on television, but he didn't hear the name or the story. Interesting. He felt ready to go. No dreams last night. But . . . hell of a lot of dead people in there.

They dressed him in a pair of gray pants and a gray shirt and gave him a gray raincoat and they were all quiet about it, and everything fit fine and he himself decided to shut up, although it had been a long time since he had talked to anybody. They took him down out of the hospital and put him in a car with three serious, silent people who said nothing, just asked him how he felt, and he felt rather nervous, but he said he felt fine. It rained a bit: the windshield wipers flickered; the trees were bending. Then the rain stopped and the sky cleared, and they came out into open ground and stopped.

He saw squads of armed soldiers, all in battle dress. It was like an eerie movie. But they were real. They watched him get out of the car and he felt all the eyes turn toward him like cameras, and he sniffed and felt anxious to get out of there and delighted and amazed. He saw Richard Ring.

A tall man, calm-faced, still wearing a tie: a wet tie. He'd been out in the rain. He came forward formally, put out his hand. Nick shook it. Ring asked him if he'd had a pleasant night, if everything was satisfactory, and Nick said, "Sure, let's go."

Ring said, "Must say again. You could die. Right soon."

"Yup. Want me to sign something?"

There was an Army officer behind Ring—a palefaced, nervous man, two stars—General. Major General? The General handed forth a paper. "Read that, son. Take your time."

Ring repeated, "Take your time."

He squinted up, held out a hand, no raindrop came.

Nick signed the thing without reading it. What the hell. "Let's go."

Ring said, "You didn't read it."

Nick shrugged. Ring said, from studious eyes, "We've put an insurance coverage on you. As a matter of detail. Because of your service to your country. Why not read that?"

"That's okay."

"But, who do you want to leave it to?"

Nick said nothing.

"You have a family. What's the address?"

Nick hadn't seen any of them, not in years. When he was sent back to the hospital in this town for recuperation after the big wreck he had mailed one letter to his brother, but his brother had not come down. Nick said, "My closest friend is an old cop. But . . . he's in town."

"Well, we need the address of somebody. Just in case. What the hell. Nothing will happen. But we need an address."

Nick thought of the old cop: Joe Ehrlich. Approaching retirement. He was there to care for Nick after the death of Nick's parents. That last night . . . he would have been somewhere near the jail. Yes. Doing some paperwork on lawsuits. So he was probably inside the jail. Good man. Have to look for him. Maybe . . . always possible. Nick said, "Tell you what. I'll give you the address of my uncle Fred."

A nice guy. Long time ago. Never see him anymore, but he was a good man when you were a kid. Dreamy. Kind of dopey. But nice.

The address went down on paper. Ring said again, strain in his face, "Hope to Christ we don't have to pay this. Hell, we won't. You just go on in and come back, damned fast. Just look into the physics area. Use the detecting system we've got here. Look."

Ring pointed at a gray car, took Nick toward it. A Chevvy? Nick saw a green-lighted radio on the dash, a mike fixed under it. Light rain was on the window. To the right, a series of gauges. Ring said, "This is rather a special car. We've, ah, taken some time with it. I doubt any problems. Well, you're a pilot, of course. I assume you're familiar with radios, etcetera."

"Um."

"We're giving you two spares," Ring said. He reached out of the car and an officer handed him a small black box, with an antenna lightly sticking out. Ring handed it to Nick, told him how to use it. Ring said, "That's an MR 114. No problem with the range. You can take that by hand whenever you leave the car. There's a spare in the trunk. Now. No problem? Fine. Now, as to the spares." The officer handed a pistol, handle first, to Ring, and Ring took it, opened the barrel, checked it, saw that it was loaded, gave that to Nick—a heavy thing—a box of shells. "A .357 Magnum," Ring said. "Just carry it with you. Very handy. May be, oh, wild dogs, we don't know. But we think it's a good idea. What do you think?"

"It's heavy."

"It's also loaded."

"Um." Nick laid the thing on the seat beside him. Ring said, a little more cheerily, pointing, "There's also a rifle in the back seat. See there?" Nick saw: blue, long-barreled. He had not hunted anything in years. Mostly what he liked was to fish. Ring said, with growing pleasure, "We're trying to think of anything at all you'll need. First thought is protection. This is the best we can do. Any suggestions?"

Nick shook his head. Ring eyed him, smiled slightly.

"Your record indicates you know how to shoot."

"From the air," Nick said. "From the air."

"Well." Ring chuckled. "So far: communication and protection. Always keep in touch. Never any problem. Keep your car radio constantly in touch, and if you have anything at all to say we'll be waiting for you to use the mike. We'll also be asking questions, naturally. Hope we don't overdo it. But keep in touch. Now, we have a camera."

He gave that to Nick and it was a complicated gadget that Nick slowly learned operated itself. All you had to do was point and shoot. There were two of those; they went into the back seat. Then Ring said, "We've got just about all of it. Can you think of anything? Oh, by the way, we've got some food." Two plastic bags were handed through a window, tucked into the back seat. Two large thermos jugs. Ring went down the list of foods: enough for perhaps three days. Just to be thorough. Coffee, water. Even cold Coke. Nick had to grin. Ring saw it, suddenly smiled, grimaced.

"Christ, I wish I was going with you."

"Well."

"I'm half tempted to try, but the odds are . . ."

Ring shook his head. He reached out suddenly, patted Nick on the leg.

"Okay, son. Can you think of anything?"

Nick paused, brooded, shook his head.

Ring put his arm out of the car, waved.

Nick saw a long gray bar of iron was across the black wet road. There were soldiers on both sides, military vehicles, with silvery sides, machine-gun-armed, on both sides of the road. The long gray bar began to rise, like the border bar into No Man's Land.

Ring said, "Start the car. I'll go with you a little way."

Nick started the engine, put her into gear. Faces were watching him. He moved under the bar down a wet black road. On the other side of the bar there was no one, nothing, no movement. Ring said, "Go up there to the top of the rise. Stop there. How does it feel?"

"Fine. I'll be fine. It runs fine."

A gray sky. A black wet road running slow and straight and narrow up a long slope, a fence to the right, a grass field empty of cows dipping down toward a grove of trees. Trees to the left, pine trees and oak and Spanish moss. It began to rain again, slowly. Nick turned the wiper on. Nothing moved anywhere, not even birds.

They moved up toward the top of the slope. There was a white house to the right, a small white house with a tractor nearby in the open, wet, in what may have been a cornfield. Ring said, "Better stop here."

His face was wet: he was perspiring. He had an instrument in his hand, was peering at it. Nick stopped. Ring sat there, gazing up the road. All you could see was the top of the rise, gray sky on the other side. The rain was increasing. Nick said, "This as far as you go?"

Ring nodded. His wet face radiated a sudden gloom.

"Wish to hell I could go with you."

Nick waited. Ring said, "Well, keep in touch." He opened the door, squinted up into the rain, looked down the road, then back at Nick. He said stiffly, "Hope to God there's no trouble."

"Don't worry about it."

"The gadgets we have in the car . . . will be sending out information. So we'll be following you pretty close. Anyway."

Ring thrust out a wet hand. "Take care, buster."

Nick said, "I'll see you."

Ring was out of the car, stood there in the rain, put his hands in his pockets. Nick put the car into gear. Ring tapped his forehead, an automatic salute.

"Keep in touch," he said.

Nick waved, stepped on the gas. He moved into the Zone.

He did not feel it for a long moment. It was very quiet in the car and very gray in the sky and the road was black and calm and empty, and there was a quiet sound from the engine and the patient thump of the wipers, and then he saw a black bird come out of the sky on the left and cross over him, flying to the right in the light rain, disappearing behind the trees. It was the first motion. And then he felt the current.

It came slowly, very slowly. He searched, feeling an eerie thing impossible to describe. Then suddenly ahead he could see sunlight on the road and he went around a bend and he was in the sunlight, strong and warm, with the rain still falling, and at the moment he drove into open country, wide open on both sides of the road, empty fields on both sides, empty and flat and brown and green and motionless, stretching out all the way to the horizon on both sides, and the sun shining from a blue sky to the east, but the rain still falling, and he felt for one long engraving moment that he was truly alone in the world, the whole world, and that the black road was endless. Then he saw a horse. It was one black horse a long way off, standing by a fence. He saw the motion of the horse's head but he could hear no sound. He thought: bet it's talking. Wonder who's fed it?

Then he knew nobody had fed it. He did not stop. No time now. When? He saw a flock of birds in the clear blue sky to the south: crows, moving west. Motion was beginning. But no people. He saw: a car ahead. Parked by the side of the road. He drove that way slowly, quietly, expecting dead bodies. A blue car, wet with rain. He saw: nothing. The car was empty. He was pleased at that. He relaxed. He drove down the winding road, heading south. The rain stopped. The ground ahead was clear and bright. He began to see mud in splotches on the road, and clouds of wet leaves that had blown onto the road and remained there, because nothing had come this way. He drove on and on through empty country: trees and fields and occasionally cows, and then suddenly one herd of cows saw him and started to run toward him, bawling, and he could hear the sound through the closed window and it chilled him; they were hungry. Then he saw two bodies.

He saw hands reaching up out of the grass.

He slowed.

A bearded man on his back, by the side of the road. Palms up, elbows on the ground. Gray and brown and dead. Then there were tree roots and a pine tree near him and two long legs in jeans lying there, the rest of the body behind the pine, and bags on the ground there—hikers?—and a hat down over the only face, a torn hat, two wanderers dead by the side of the road. Nick moved on by.

A gas station. Car parked in front with the hood open. No one visible. But a yellow glow inside the station. A light on inside. Nick slowed, stopped, looked. Nothing moved. He did not want to go into the station. He heard the voice of Ring: "How you doing, boy?"

"Fine. Fine."

"What do you see?"

"Nothing. A couple of bodies."

"Where?"

"Dead bodies alongside the road. Hikers, I think. Must have been sleeping. Wait a minute."

Nick came around a bend and the trees were close to the side of the narrow road, and there was a car on the road, a black car, front wheels off the road. Through the back window Nick saw a head on the driver's seat rest. He slowed, drove to the left, looking.

"I see one. Wait a minute."

"What do you see?"

A man resting in a car, head back slightly, staring upward. Face gray and a smudged greenish glow: unreal. But real, all right, real when you looked. A dead man. Stone dead. Thoroughly dead. Mouth open. Dirty teeth. Head straight back against the seat rest, long sharp gray teeth. Ring was talking. Nick said, "You see a few dead, here and there."

"No motion?"

"Nothing but a few cows. And birds. And there's a dog out there."

He saw a small black dog running across a field, moving faster than he had seen tame dogs move, leaping, hurdling bushes, vanishing into wet woods.

"Nobody alive?"

"Animals."

Nick saw another row of bawling cows. He saw wide desperate eyes. Ought to stop someday and feed the poor bastards. He felt a clutch in his stomach. Hell with this. No way to feed them all. Take days and days and food after food to feed them all. He speeded up. Came around a bend and passed three cars parked close together alongside the road, and then one long big truck, a truck that towed cars: Mercurys, and Nick didn't look inside more than a second or two, just saw motionless faces and frozen fingers clawing like weak statues. Ring said, "You see no living people?"

"No."

"Well. What's your mileage?"

"Ah. It says twenty-nine. Um. Was it zero when I started?"

"Yep. You're more than halfway. Calmly now. Take it calmly. How fast do you drive? Watch it, the road could be messy."

68

"It is. It's dirty. There're leaves and mud and sometimes small branches. Christ."

"What's the matter?"

"It's different, man, it's not the same."

"What's different?"

"It's unoccupied."

"Well, take your time."

He came into a small valley. He saw rows of trailers, the things they called mobile homes. He saw the cars parked nearby and white cloth blowing on rope lines and some of the cloth on the ground and caught on trees and wet mud on the clothes, and he saw a pack of dogs, four, five, standing by a trailer looking at him, motionless, watching, and he drove looking for a living soul but saw no one. He had moments of awe. A new world. He suddenly treasured the .357 Magnum, on the seat by him. He remembered: a potent gun. Old friend once, old Joe, the cop, shot the thing through car engines when he wanted to stop them.

He saw smoke ahead, gray smoke rising on a clear day: long round heavy smoke, blowing east. He saw more birds. He was coming to town.

Somewhere far off was a fire. No mistaking the heavy smoke. Far away, behind trees, the rising houses. He came down the first long string of houses: little white houses, white brick, a construction site, neat and small and tidy and empty . . . but there were dogs again, a pack of dogs moving across somebody's yard. He came around one bend and saw the big roofs up ahead, the big buildings on the rise above the river: two banks and the two hotels and part of the University, and then in the center of the street he saw a pack of dogs and a dead animal. A cow. A dead cow. Stomach torn away and the dogs eating and tearing. They did not see him come. They were tearing at the cow on a street on the edge of town, and he wondered how the cow got there—it must have broken away and wandered and the dogs had nothing to eat and they were over it now and fighting and eating and one saw him and he saw wild fangs and he turned left in to a quiet street, and there ahead was the tall white hospital, and beyond that the smoke from a source of fire, and then he was at the crest overlooking the main part of town, down toward the river, and it was all there suddenly, all the rows of buildings, and the big ones like white blocks, and the pipe columns up from the paper plant but no smoke there; the smoke was from a group of houses off to the left, something burning heavily, thoroughly with black smoke, but he could see no fire. He stopped the car and sat there with the doors closed and the engine running, staring.

There was a red light at the corner in front of him. It blinked, turned yellow, turned green. Nick said, "Be god-damned."

"What's the matter?" Ring's voice, very fast.

"The power's still on. Don't see anybody. Not a soul. Except hungry dogs. But the power's still on here. Some of the power. The lights still work."

"All right. That's maybe normal. Probably part of it's automatic, will run without service until they refuel it. The power source is inside the Zone. Don't worry on that. What do you see?"

Nick breathed, watched. Silence. White brick. Walls. Smoke. Far off a few dogs ran down an empty street. No cars. Not even a parked car. He said, "Empty. The town is empty."

"Can you take some pictures?"

"There's just some smoke. And dogs. And a few birds. And the damn lights go on and off. But not a damn thing moves. Smoke. Somebody left something burning."

"Be careful of live wires."

"What?"

"Maybe there is some live electricity. Think on that. Keep your eyes open. If you step on the wrong thing . . ."

"Never thought of that."

70

"And watch the dogs."

"I'm near the hospital. Listen."

"What?"

"I think I'll check it out."

"Why?"

Nick put the car into gear, drove slowly toward the white building, which was tall and old and filled with memories. Still no motion. He remembered the morning on the front steps with Rachel. Dead now at the airport. Dead for a long time. A beautiful girl. Dead for a long, long time. Will look like . . . don't want to see.

He stopped in front of the hospital. No cars parked there, very few in the parking lot. It came in the middle of the night. Ring said, "What's on your mind?"

"Well, there may be some poor bastard in there."

Silence. Nick said, "I was in there once with broken legs and I couldn't move and maybe there's some poor bastard in there now who can't get out."

"But you haven't seen anybody."

"Only a few minutes. I'll take a look."

Nick was in command and knew it. He had all his life been an independent man. Ring said, "Take a gun with you."

"All right."

Nick took the .357 and went out the door and up the steps. He went back and turned off the engine of the car. Want that to run. Then he went back inside.

There were two dead bodies in the foyer. He did not look at them closely. He found a mess at the reception desk: papers spread on the floor, very messy. And there was money. He knelt. Dollar bills. Five, six. He had Ring's little radio in his hand and told him about that. He said, "It doesn't figure. Do you think somebody went flaky?"

"Possible. Be careful. Very careful. Listen, you think this is necessary?"

"I know just the one floor. I'll check that. And if I hear anything . . ."

Nick took a deep breath. He yelled, *"Hey!"* He paused. *"Anybody here?"*

He paused. He went up to the second floor.

Silence.

He was passing: the newborn babies.

God.

He hadn't meant that.

He saw: rows of newborn babies.

Motionless in the crib. The color was death. He turned away, leaned against the wall. Hadn't thought of this. Rows of dead babies. He stood there for a moment, Ring's radio in his hand. Ring couldn't hear him well; he couldn't hear Ring. He said loudly, sick in the chest, "Oh, my God." Then he saw one baby that was pink.

He stared.

He ran that way. *Pink face.* Eyes closed. Pink hands.

But.

No breath.

He went around the edge, in the door, the forbidden door. He went up to the crib.

In the midst of the dead babies, from which there was no real odor, just a feeble smell, a minor smell, a blessedly minor smell, there was the one pink, rested, patient face.

Which was not breathing.

Still tears on the face.

It had lived in the crib, with no one to care for it, for almost five days.

But was now dead.

He checked the pulse.

Dead.

Always a chance.

He tried to move the body.

Dead. Not quite pink. The color just contrasted with the

others. This one had lived for a little while longer. This one had been immune. This one died through lack of care.

Nineteen. He would have been nineteen.

Nick went outside and sat down for a moment in a chair. He felt as bad as he had ever felt. He was not fond of babies and he had never known one he really cared for and worried about, but that one small newborn thing in there.

He went back into the hall and yelled.

No answer.

He went to the next hall and yelled.

No answer.

He looked in a few of the rooms.

The dead bodies sat there, lay there asleep.

This is the way the world ends. Not with a bang . . .

He came back downstairs and out into the open air. He sat on the concrete steps, holding the gun in hand. He tucked it in his belt. He had never seen a newly born dead baby. He did not know what it was about it that got to him. He thought: well, the kid never knew. . . . He sat there. This is the way the world ends. . . . He heard the voice of Ring. He was asking about odor. Nick said, "Not much odor."

"That's what we've learned. How is it for you? Is it bearable?"

"Sure."

"Really? No bad side effects?"

"Really not bad. You can hardly smell anything. I found one inside who stayed alive for a while. Didn't die with the others."

"What?"

"Just a baby. If there'd been somebody around to help him . . ."

Ring was silent.

"Number nineteen," Nick said.

Ring did not answer. Nick could sense: patience. Nick said, "Must be somebody else."

73

"Possibly."

"I'm going over to the jail."

"Do you have to?"

"Yep. Got a friend there. I'd like to see him. Also, they may have somebody locked up there who's still alive and starving to death, so I'll just see; it's just down the corner."

"All right, but listen, son, better not waste time, better . . ."

"I'm not wasting time."

Nick got back in the car and turned her on and swung down the block toward the jail he'd known so well, the jail that was the home of ancient Joe, the gentle cop, the cop with a battered arm and a damaged heart who'd taken care of Nick through the long, long months after his parents died . . . there had been nights he would remember all the rest of his life when he'd sat in there with the damaged man who told him to hang on, hang on, and one night gave him some good Scotch, very good Scotch, and put him to sleep and then let him sleep in a cell, and he'd come awake in the morning a little bit better, a little more sane, so he drove down the streets, with windows open on a sunny, motionless day, down dusty streets with leaves in the streets and the walkways, and he heard music.

He slowed: a woman singing. No: a yell. Then he heard a loud commercial. Rattling away. Then a placid speech: laughter. He stopped. Chat chat. Selling something? No. A quiz show? He said to Ring, "I hear something."

He stopped the car, got out. He knew: television program. It rattled away. Some man probing and squeezing and delighted war whoops in a tinny background. It came from a small house with a small porch. Nick said, "Goddamn. A TV set is running."

"Do you see anybody?"

"Not a soul. But. Shall I check it?"

"Well, just take a minute. If you can find a friend."

Nick hopped out of the car, the motor left running, and popped up the steps to the back door of the small house. He knocked. No answer.

The quiz switched to music, an organ. Nick tried the door, it opened. He saw: a dark room. Curtains drawn. But there in a small living room he saw a TV picture, slowly sliding upward, always upward, and a man hugging a girl who had just won and was crying, and Nick saw a large chair facing the TV set and a hand on the arm of the chair, and the hair of a head, and knew instantly that the man was dead, could smell him slightly but not terribly, and Nick went forward to turn off the TV set. To Ring he said, into the hand radio, "Nothing. A fella in here stayed up late to watch the late show and fell asleep in the chair, and never . . ."

Nick was looking out the window.

He saw a mass of dogs.

They were herding.

Twenty. Thirty.

Dobermans. The front door was slightly open. Nick ran, got there, slammed it shut; something hit the other side. He heard an intense scream from some dogs. He looked at the windows. All down. God bless. But . . . in his pocket. No gun. He said, "I left the goddamned thing in the car."

He stood by the window. The dogs were gathered in a mass. He saw bloody faces, remembered the cow. He thought: Jesus Christ. Who feeds them now?

You do.

Goddamn it. He picked up the hand radio. He said, "You know what I am? I'm a goddamned idiot, that's what I am."

Ring asked what happened. He told him. All the windows were down. He had some time. Was . . . this why he saw no other humans? Thank God they couldn't get into the hospital. All right, old buddy, you nitwit, how the hell do you get out of here?

Maybe they've got a gun.

Please God, a gun.

Ring was saying, "Careful, take your time. Think on it."

"Maybe they've got a gun here."

"Yes, but listen, we can help you. We've got an armored vehicle. We can send it into where you are—it'll take some time, we'll have to arrange it—but we can get it ready and send it in and it can kill the dogs, if we can find where you are."

"How the hell do you find me?"

"By radio. Don't overuse the radio. We'll home in on you. Now, be careful. Is there an upstairs?"

"Yep."

"Why not go upstairs and get yourself barricaded? There may be a lot of big dogs. Sorry. I should have thought of that."

"Maybe there's a gun up there."

"Well, get yourself safe. It'll take us a little time to get things set up. Dammit! We'll need a TV camera and a guide, but we've got them, so don't worry, just play it cool. But. How do you feel? You feel anything . . . wrong?"

"Listen, if I feel lousy, dammit, I'll let you know. What I'm going to do now, please God, is find me a gun."

"Right. But play it cool. *Cool.* No chances. Because I tell you, laddie, the dogs can be very dangerous and hard to stop and I hope to God . . ."

Nick hopped into the kitchen. Nothing. There was a garage out back, but he could not get back out there and he didn't think they would keep a gun there anyway. He saw new faces, the teeth of a big gray German shepherd, the foolish faces of frantic little dogs, even a dachshund. He thought: the dachshunds need to eat; they'll eat the scraps. Goddamnit.

He hopped up the stairs. A bedroom: two dead children. He turned away in rage, despair. Another bedroom: the dead mother. Face against the pillow dead five days. Ghastly.

He stopped, waited, took a breath of bad air, went in, opened the closet door, saw: a shotgun.

He held it lovingly in his hands, opened it lovingly, stared lovingly into empty barrels.

Ancient, double-barreled. Worn. *But.*

Serviceable.

Two good shots.

Will kill two from above. From the top windows. Oh, excellent.

If you can find a slug.

Well, he must have a slug.

But maybe he only kills birds.

Please God. Not birds.

There were no shells in the closet.

He searched all through the small upstairs.

Nothing.

He thought: if there's anything, it's in the kitchen, in the cupboard. Sensible, sensible.

He hopped downstairs. He could hear scratching at the door, an unreal whine. He went into the kitchen.

Not in the cupboard.

Not under the cupboard.

But in the wall where they kept a vacuum cleaner, a box of shells.

One box of shot.

To kill the birds.

And this: four slugs.

Just four.

He has hunted the deer.

Twelve-gauge slugs.

Four.

Nick loaded two.

He went across the room from the sleeping dead man and sat there with a loaded shotgun.

Four?

Worth a try. You can always shoot from upstairs and see what happens.

He told Ring about that on the radio. Ring warned him to be damned careful. Nick said, "You know what I think? I think most of them will run like hell."

"But. Most of them."

"Well, how long will it take you? How long do I have to sit here with the dead folks?"

"A few hours. We . . . will have to rush to get it set up by nightfall. May even take until morning."

"Oh, the hell with that. Look, I'll head upstairs, and fire—wait a minute—one bird shot to spread 'em out and one slug to kill one and see what happens—and then if they break, I'll move out front, and all I have to do is get a few feet to the car."

"Well."

"Might's well try."

"Let me know as soon as . . ."

"Well, I can't hold everything in these hands. I'll listen, stick the radio in the pocket."

"All right, but dammit . . ."

"I will."

Nick leaped back up the stairs. He found a window in the woman's bedroom very near her body but with nothing outside it, no way for anything to be standing there able to get in, and he could see all the dogs forming out there, several big and oddly stiff and different, as if they weren't even really dogs, but creatures invented for an eerie movie. One was a Doberman, large and sleek and dark and with something about the face of it that was instinctively dangerous, and it was poised at the foot of the steps, motionless, searching, waiting, poised, twitching the mouth, the teeth. Nick opened the window slowly, quietly, but the eyes swung toward him suddenly and he heard the raw howls, the odd howls, the howls almost of sick animals, and he tucked one

slug in one chamber and one round of shot in the other
barrel and aimed the slug at the big Doberman and blasted.

Twelve gauge jolts the shoulder. But the shot hit the
Doberman in the head. Pieces of the dog's head flew. The
thing fell over. There was a wild commotion. Dogs leaped.
Nick fired the bird shell into a mass. He heard screaming,
saw jumping, all of it too fast. And then they were running.
He saw most of the small ones were gone. But there were big
ones there, backing, the teeth all bared. Nick loaded another
slug, killed a big Shepherd. He loaded the last two slugs. The
dogs were running down the street, away from him. He
hopped down the stairs, no time to wait, looked out the front
window. The porch was clear. He was loaded. No damn dog
would hide behind anything.

Or would it?

A Doberman.

You could wait?

All night.

How long will you last?

Until you throw up.

But . . . you feel okay.

Well.

He cocked both barrels, swung the door open.

Nothing.

Once I get in the car.

It isn't twenty yards away.

Do you see anything?

Not a damned thing.

Well.

Let's go.

He walked out the open door with the cocked shotgun in
his arms.

Down the street he saw one black dog waiting.

And then it ran suddenly away.

He stepped over the body of the dead Doberman. Parts

of the dead dog's head were on the car. He opened the door and got in and sat there with the doors closed and the windows up and shuddered for a moment, then contacted Ring.

"Everything all right?"

"Whee."

"Don't *ever* leave that car without a gun. Understand?"

"Check."

"That .357 is quick and strong and repeatable, and at close range, listen, stick it in your pocket."

"Right."

"Now. How do you feel?"

"Weary."

"That all?"

"Yes. I'm okay. I feel fine."

"Have some coffee."

"Good idea. No need for wine."

"Listen. I'm . . . damn glad you're okay."

"Me too."

"Well, we'll try to do better. But kid, please, for all of us as well as yourself, please, be careful."

"Right." Nick drank. Good, good coffee. "This is good stuff," he said. "What kind of stuff is this?"

"Ah, hell, I don't know. Wait. Maxwell House."

"Good stuff. Well, I think I'll get moving."

"Where to?"

"The jail."

"Are you sure?"

"Yep."

"You've already taken a lot of time. How do you feel?"

"Scared. Weak. Stupid. But okay. I'll be okay. And I want to go by . . . just for a minute."

"All right. But keep the gun in your hand. See any more dogs?"

"No. Be damned." He chuckled. Hell of a world. Empty

80

world. Jesus. Everybody else worries about mugging, burglary, kidnapping, terrorists—me—in an empty world, I'm chased by some goddamn dogs.

He started the car, drove off down the quiet street. There were many trees on the street and thick leaves overhead, and the sun came through in small yellow dots on a quiet empty neighborhood, no cars visible anywhere. Nick thought: what if it had happened in the daytime?

He came down to the jail.

It was old red brick. It had been there since the turn of the century, improved, improved, but the outer part red and ancient. He stopped there and took the .357 and loaded it and saw no dogs but took it in one hand and the radio in the other and tucked the box of cartridges in his pocket before he left the car. He went up the stairs and suddenly felt strikingly tired. He got inside and found a chair by the glassed-in sergeant's desk and sat down and chatted with Ring. Then he sat there, wishing for more coffee, and then he shouted but there was no answer. And then suddenly he didn't want to go upstairs. He didn't want to see his friend's body. He was tiring of this day and the silence and the fear of the dogs. And yet after a moment of sitting, a moment of rest, the stubbornness was back and the old independence, and he said, "*Anybody home?*" and began to wander. He heard no sound, nothing. He thought it was empty. But there were a few cells down there and he just looked in, just for a moment, not planning on seeing them all, and he saw feet on the floor in one, under a blanket, and then he saw a girl sitting in the next one, looking at him, with wide black eyes.

She had long black hair and wide black eyes and she was sitting on a cot with a blanket hugged in her arms, staring at him.

She was alive, all right. She had one hand to her chest: her heart was beating. She was rather pretty. She was terrified.

81

Nick said, "How are you?"

She stared at him, blinked, held her throat.

Nick said gently, "You're okay, kid. You're okay."

His mind said: *twenty.*

* * *

Armitage said, "You should have given him a TV camera."

They sat under a dark sky in gnawed silence. Ring smoked. Armitage said wistfully, "Why don't you give him one next time?"

"If there is a next . . ."

"Hey, Mr. Ring? I've found somebody."

The voice came out of the speaker. Ring jumped, pinched the mike.

"What's happening?"

"Well, there's a girl in here. And she's alive. And seems okay. Only she's locked up, and she sits there, and the poor kid, boy, it must have been a hell of a time."

Pause. Ring said, "A girl?"

"Yep. She's . . . about twenty, I guess. Poor kid. She's been in there, holy cow, *five days.* With nobody else here. I mean, the place is *empty.* And the poor kid, she just looks at me and won't talk. I've backed away a little bit and she's just sitting there, a long way away, and sometimes she won't look at me."

Ring swore to himself. After a moment Nick said, "She's been *alone* in here, locked, for five days. I think . . . I ought to feed her something. Look, why not some medical advice? You have a doctor there can help me? I can get things for her, and hand 'em in through the bars."

Ring looked at Armitage. After a moment Armitage jumped, grunted, nodded. "I know who to get. Be here in a few minutes. Right." He moved off. Ring said through the microphone, "I'm getting you a doctor. Everything all right? No problem?"

"No problem. Poor kid. She's . . . kinda cute. Wonder

why she's in here. Well, can't ask. Listen, another thing. How do I get her out of the cell? I don't know how. I don't know if she'll come out."

Ring looked at Armitage's main aide: a Major. The man blinked, jumped, moved off. Ring said to Nick, "We'll do what we can. It must be . . . electrical. Maybe if you'll just look around." Ring looked down at his watch. Already after noon. But nothing to say. He could not push the younger man.

Nick said, "I'll try to talk a little bit. I'll move in. Listen, I'll be waiting to hear from you and a doctor, but I think what I'll do is just hop out and get some coffee and Coke and some sandwiches out of my own kit, and see if the kid will eat something, because she must be hungry. How could she eat, locked up in there for five days with nobody out here? Well."

"Watch yourself," Ring said.

"Right ho, buddy. I'll keep in touch."

Ring put down his mike. Armitage was already coming with a little man in uniform. Ring stood up, stretched, took a deep breath, shook his head. Take a walk, old soul. Take a walk. The doctor said into the mike: "Hello, there. Hello?" Ring walked away. At that moment, in fine, light, misty drops, it began to rain.

The radio truck with the tall antenna was parked in an open field by the road gate to the Zone. There were only a few officers near the truck. The troops had been moved back to a field to the north, all but sentries quartered along the fence, but the field back there was dotted with tents and there were blocks of soldiers sitting there, most of them eating. It was quiet and there was no wind. Ring walked out on the wet road, off by himself, away from the gate. He had been all his life a patient man, but something was slipping now. He rubbed his face. He looked suddenly south, toward the invisible Wall. He felt a gathering anger.

"Well, she's been alive for *five days*. Amazing."

83

Corelli. Ring looked. The little Italian had followed him, was grinning, shaking his wet head. He said happily, "Now, *that's* good. That's really very good. First *good* news. If that girl has been there five days and is still alive, I think our boy will last it out, don't you?"

Ring lighted a cigarette.

Corelli said, "Well, one or two other facts. Didn't want to bother you while you were busy."

"What?"

"Nothing important. We got a little word on A. M. Shepherd."

Ring looked at the little man, the patient face, the wide, dark, happy eyes. Corelli said cheerily, "Nothing much. Nothing important. But we *did* find out that he arrived in Jefferson, on a trip in from Rome, Italy, two days before the, ah, lethal accident. He, ah, has not been known to come out. *Yet.* So he's still in there. And, ah, the reason for his visit was to see a friend of his, a man named David Huston, who teaches, ah, *taught,* at the University there. Young man, ah, thirty-four. Was once a student of Shepherd's a few years back, at, ah, Berkeley. And what we've been able to find is that Shepherd came in there to see Mr., ah, Huston, and apparently to check into some genetic experiments. Huston was interested in something called the, ah"—Corelli looked at a soggy paper, squinted—"uh, something called the, ah, *Chang Po Effect.* Whatever that is. No evidence. Of any kind. Except that it probably had something to do with genetics."

"Chang Po."

"That's the, ah, word they've written."

"Chinese?"

Corelli blinked, put a hand to his mouth. Ring said, "Any connection?"

"I never thought of that. The Chinese factor."

"Well, think on it. What was happening in that town?"

Corelli shook his head, raised empty palms. "I've found

nothing. Absolutely nothing. No major grants of any kind. No sophisticated equipment. No research at that University which could possibly lead to major radiation. But then . . . this thing is . . . unique. I tell you, that man Shepherd . . ."

"All right. Tell me something about Shepherd."

"Ah. Well, he makes the scalp crawl. But of course he's dead, or we would have heard."

"What do you *know* about him?"

"Awfully sorry. He . . . I really don't know anything. A brilliant man. Thoroughly brilliant. Far smarter than I, of course. But some men thought he was laughable, and believe me he was *not*."

"Goddammit, for once, just once, get to the point."

Corelli saw the look on Ring's face.

"Well, he . . . Shepherd wanted to change mankind. That's what he said he was in the genetics business to do. To change mankind into something . . . better. And some of the things . . ."

"Mr. Ring?"

A young blond aide, saluting.

"Sir? Excuse me, sir, but there is a call for you, from Mr. Hiller, in Washington. Top priority, sir."

He held up a small black box.

"You can take it here, sir, if you like." He gave Ring the radio, saluted, backed away a few yards, stood there, at ease. Corelli started to back away. Ring said, "Wait a minute. Hang around." Then into the radio he said, "Ring here. Go ahead."

Hiller wanted to know what was going on. Ring told him about Nick being in town all morning and the discovery of a live girl and a dead baby. He never got to the dogs. Hiller wanted to know when Nick was going to get moving, and Ring didn't know, and then Hiller said, swearing, that this thing was getting rather sticky. Ring agreed, waited. Hiller said, "Listen, I may have to send you a Russky. One or two. Rather privately. You understand."

"Russian?"

"They're nervous as hell. They want to . . . see for themselves. Test it themselves. They're really very nervous. You follow me?"

"Yes."

"This is sticky. We don't want to play games. If I send them down, you show them what you know now. But nothing new. Talk to me first. But now, what's coming up? What can I tell the President?"

"Sorry. The kid's our only hope right now. The radiation continues."

"I think, goddammit, that it was done on purpose."

"Possible."

"What do you think?"

"I don't know."

"After five goddamn days?"

"If you want to send somebody else."

"Christ, no! I wouldn't trust anybody else. But listen, everybody's rather nervous. I've got to talk to the press. But listen, time may be getting short. We may have to hit that town to keep the peace."

"All right."

"I'm sitting here. Call me. I may be sending somebody. Listen, *they* need reassurance. This could be a very dangerous weapon, very dangerous, and we have to know what it is and reassure everybody that it was only an accident, which I hope to God it was, but I don't think it was . . . oh, what the hell, call me when you can."

He was gone. Ring thought: what does *he* know?

The man would know things that he might not think Ring needed to know. Ring was only the tool. Up near the Zone. Ring felt suddenly violently empty. He took the small black box and flipped it to the young officer. At that moment he saw another officer coming his way, running. He stopped, saluted. The young face was tight, strange: different. Ring thought: scared? The officer said, "Sir? Could you come up, please? Come this way here?"

He pointed toward the gate. Ring said, "What's the matter?"

"The radiation, sir."

"What's up?"

"It seems to be moving."

At that moment Ring saw a man break from the side of the radio truck and come running back down through the field, running away. But no one else ran. They all stood there like dark wet statues, in dead silence, looking toward the Wall, and for a long moment Ring had no idea, then it began to come, and he broke forward toward the gate. Faces turned toward him. Blank faces: a nightmare of wet men with death in their eyes. He felt his skin prickle.

The current.

He saw Armitage, a meter in his hand. Ring said, "What is happening?"

"It's begun to move."

"Lethal yet?"

"Not yet. But."

"Is the wind blowing it?"

Armitage shook his head. "Don't think so. Radio says it's spreading everywhere."

His face had gone white. If the thing was coming, they would all be dead in a little while. Armitage said in a high voice, "Report by radio from the other side. The stuff is spreading out slowly. Can you feel it? Perfect circle. It's not blowing, it's spreading. It's"—he blinked at the meter, held it closer to his eyes, wiped his wet face—"it's getting stronger."

Ring could begin to feel it. It came like a fever. For a long second he stood there. Then he saw men begin to break. A few ran away. He heard trucks starting. There was heavier rain. The soldiers up by the fence were beginning to back away. He thought: will running help?

What else can you do?

A voice said, "Sir, we want to know . . ." The voice broke.

Ring said, "All right. We have a few minutes. Only thing to do is move out. Get back away as far away as you can, as soon as you can. Get in the trucks and pull back fast. Move everybody. Keep some order. Waste no time. We have time. But move. Don't panic. But *move*. Move to where you can no longer feel it and we'll see."

But there was no way to calm it now. They were breaking, running, driving away. He could see them breaking back from the tents, on foot running away from the oncoming Wall into the far trees. Armitage stood there: freckles like red dots against gray skin. Ring said, "I guess . . . we'll just go. Good luck, John."

They began to walk. Ring thought at last, hell man, better run. Always a chance. It may not spread far. It may not be thick enough to kill you. Run away. Run as long as you can. Run, goddammit, and stay alive.

No way to go by truck: the road was a jammed, wrecked, already burning mess. He ran off the road in the rain. A short way down the road he felt no radiation. He felt a blessed wondrous calm, good clean air, good cold air, but he went on running to the north, leaving the gate and fence-posts and guns across the road, and a field of white tents silent in a silent rain.

FOUR

The radio went dead. No one took the time to tell Nick Tesla why. It went dead. He sat asking questions, waiting for an answer. After a while he went out and tried the one in the car. He got nothing. He came back in and sat on a chair in front of the girl's cell, and she would not look at him. She sat with the blanket over her head. He could hear her begin to cry. He said plaintively, "Gee whiz, lassie, I wish I could help. But I don't know what the hell to do. Listen, why don't you eat something? I've got this stuff here."

He put in one sandwich through the bars, laid it on the floor, put in one cup of Coke. The doctor had said something about medicine and Nick had written it down, but the food was the most important, and the nerve problem was quite a problem, because the girl would not look at him, or talk, or even listen to him. He sat for an hour. Every now and then he asked the girl if she'd mind eating something, just to make him feel better, and she didn't move under the blanket and he thought she might be dead, and then she moved, and he saw she'd been asleep. Her face was stark white. Her eyes were sick.

He said coaxingly, seriously, "Now, listen, lassie, this is an elderly buddy talking, and what I'm telling you, child, is that you better eat now, because you'll feel better. Will you please? Here's a roast beef sandwich, no kidding, a good one. What do you want on it? It's got salt and all that. You want Worcestershire sauce or something? I can find ketchup. But eat something. I tell you, I'm scared, honey. Please eat something. Make me feel better. Please."

She closed her eyes, sat there.

He stood up.

"All right," he said, "I'll tell you what I'll do. If I'm scaring you, I'll just get out of here, okay? And you go ahead and eat something. But I won't bother you anymore."

He walked out of the room. Maybe with him gone . . . because from the look on her face his presence scared hell out of her. But then, if she sat there for five days and saw *nobody* . . . how would *you* go through that, laddie?

Not well.

Go upstairs, look for Joe.

No.

He did not want to see dead Joe. Joe might be alive . . . somewhere. There were bodies in various rooms and in various cells and he got the doors opened and covered them with blankets so he didn't have to look at them and he was amazed at the almost total absence of odor. That smell the first days . . . had been ominous. But he covered the bodies, and they were not serious under a blanket. He had seen many dead in his time, and the odd, unexpectable thing was that you got used to it. Maybe you were not supposed to, but you did. He saw dirty boots of a tall man sticking out from under one blanket. He was amazed at himself: he felt no real pity; he was almost embarrassed. He thought: any man's death doesn't diminish you. You are not involved in mankind. Therefore, for whom does the bell toll?

He sat out on the steps and had a cup of coffee, looking for dogs, but there were none. There was the sound of a gun firing a long way off.

A distant thump.

Must be a gun. Shotgun?

Somebody else shooting?

He sat there, looking up the quiet street. An empty town.

92

Not a dead town. It was almost as if the folks there had simply gone away. He shook his head. You're not dreaming this, Nicholas.

But there it was: broad daylight under a darkening sky and not a car in the streets nor even cars parked anywhere and nothing moving, not even dogs, not even birds, and then suddenly another gunshot, this one closer, and he felt a sense of ominous withdrawal, and he backed into the jail. There he went to work on opening more doors, and never did go upstairs to see Joe, let that one go, not quite ready for that. He finally found the box system that opened the door to the girl's cell. He stood at the end of the hall and could see the girl moving. The girl had begun to eat, and he felt delighted. He grinned. He thought: don't push any buttons. Go talk for a while.

He came slowly up the hall. She stopped eating.

She watched him, crouching. He said, trying to smile, "How're you doing?"

She said nothing.

"Go on, eat up. I've got a lot more. Anything you want? Look, there are stores down the street. I can just hop out and get anything. Except fresh meat. Don't know about fresh meat. May not be fresh anymore. But I can get cans of stuff. And frozen stuff, and I know there's a little stove over that-away, and we can heat something. So what do you want?"

He was closer. The girl crouched on the cot. He stood motionless, smiling. The girl moved. She went on eating the sandwich, watching him. Then her eyes left him, and she looked around the room.

Nick sighed, picked up the little hand radio, called, got no answer.

What the hell. Batteries?

No. Can't be.

This whole damn thing is unbelievable.

93

Open her door?

Not yet. She's not ready.

She had finished the sandwich, drank the Coke. She said nothing, sat crouched Hindu style on the bed. Nick put another sandwich through the bars: again, roast beef. He was getting hungry himself, told her he had to go out, excused himself, asked if there was anything she wanted. She shook her head. He was delighted to see her move.

"Thank you, lassie." He grinned. "See you in a few minutes."

He moved out to the car, drove off down the empty street to an empty A&P, cracked the glass door, wandered through the empty cavernous open areas picking up cans and boxes of things, crackers, beans, vegetable soup. He had no idea what to get, but he gathered a large bag and went warily back into the street, and down at the end of the road he saw sudden motion, let the bag drop, going to his pocket for the .357, and saw an ancient black Ford turn at the corner and go slowly off down the street, going away from him, pausing at a red light to look around, but not stopping, moving on and around the corner and out of sight, gone. Nick said to himself, "Well, son, get used to it. A crazy world."

But that was an old Ford. A noisy Ford. He gathered the bag, put it back in his car, drove back down an empty street to the jail. He saw nothing else move. Oh, yes: there came a small bird, a tiny bird, a swallow. It disappeared. He called again on the car radio. Nothing. He went back inside the jail. It was later now, and he was beginning to be tired. He saw the girl lying down. She sat up, gazed at him with sleepy eyes. But her face was . . . had a sweetness. Nick felt suddenly instinctively better. He smiled.

"You feel better?"

She nodded.

"Good. Great. Anything else you need, just ask."

She watched him; she looked at his hands and feet. Nick

said, "Hey, I got some crackers, things like that. Some cookies. How about that?"

She nodded.

He handed one cookie box through the bars, filled up the Coke. The Coke was fading. Don't open her door: not yet.

"I've got corn and stuff like that. What do you like? Listen, they've got a little stove up here. We can cook a TV dinner or so, if you like. Oh, and I picked up these vitamin things. You better take those. You haven't had much lately. How about that? Here."

He handed her the bottle of vitamins. The girl was eating the cookies. He saw: she was very tired. He was tired himself. He walked over to the desk in the hall and saw the chair there by the window and sat down, looking out, and there went the black Ford again, noisily up the road, out of sight. Same car. Nick sat, had the last of the coffee.

The town is not dead. There are a few here.

Nothing out there but dust and leaves and ashes and a few birds. And an occasional human being.

There's the girl. And you. And the Ford . . .

It was darker now. Still no radio contact. He turned them both off to save the batteries. He thought gloomily: goddamn, they've deserted me.

Then, no, Ring wouldn't do that. What happened?

He gazed out the window at the silent road. No car now. No sound of guns. No dogs. He thought of the Black Death. He had read a book on it not long ago. Killed people by the millions. Left a few alive. He remembered a story about one town where everybody died except one servant girl, who wandered alone through the castle, owning it. He sat thinking of that, squinted up at the sky.

Sir, if you don't mind, what the hell is the point?

In a little while the girl was asleep. Her color was better; she was healthier. Nick began to relax a little. The darkness came, the streetlights came: he saw streetlights and traffic lights gleaming and blinking. But no cars came, and no people, and no dogs, and there were no lights in any windows behind the trees. But he knew that something would move soon. Sonny, he told himself, watch out for the morning. Because Christ only knows who's dead, or what's coming, and Nick remembered the old wry religion his father used to quote, smiling, when Nick was very young: "Oh, my Lord (if there is a Lord), save my soul (if I have a soul)."

He found himself a cot in the wardroom and carried it downstairs and pitched it in the hall near the girl's cell. He thought: open her door now? You could die in the night. But if you open it, she could run away. Well, think on it.

He sat and waited. He tried Ring again. Nothing. No radio sound at all. No music. Nothing to read. He searched, found a sexy magazine. The girl woke up in the night; he gave her some heated vegetable soup, and crackers he'd arranged for himself. She still would not talk. She went back to sleep. In a silent room, in an empty world, he left the light on. He wanted music, but there was no sound but the breath of the girl, the motion of the girl. He went to sleep. He dreamed of the desert, the great yellow desert, and far out there, coming, a yellow sandstorm.

*   *   *

Ring ran up the black road. There was panic around him and trucks and cars had smashed into each other, blocking the road completely, near the trees, and the helicopters had gone and all the men were running so there was nothing to do but move out on the side of the road, down what looked like a bike path in the open grass, and then after a while Ring slowed and walked. There were very few near him now. Some were young and fast and were soon gone, and a few only walked, and some just went off the road and sat down. Ring wiped his forehead, wiped away rain and sweat, tried to feel, no pain in the stomach, no pain but some in the chest:

the heart? Running too much? Well. How long will you live?
But Ring felt no panic. He went on walking north, nothing
else to do, trying to sense the radiation. Not even any
counter, damn fool, not even a counter in your hand to know
how thick the radiation was, if there was any. So finally he
stopped by a speed sign, large and white and metallic: 55. He
leaned against the sign and waited in the darkening afternoon and tried to sense radiation, and he sensed nothing.
Could not tell, but no point in running any more. He stood
there.

No radiation.

How far have you come?

At least two miles.

It could be spreading slowly. It could be here in a
moment.

So?

He stood there by a speed sign on an empty road, under a
wet tree. The rain had slowed, was almost gone. No point in
staying here. Go somewhere and perhaps have a drink,
before the end. Go north.

He went on walking north.

A few miles later a helicopter passed overhead going back
south. He waved at it but its crew did not see him. Moments
later another one came over the road, going the same way.
Ring thought: very good—they'll have a meter aboard. A
few minutes later he came around a bend and there was an
armored car across the road, a silvery vehicle with a large
black number on it. Ring saw a helmeted officer standing
there, arms behind his back, and several armed troops. Off
to the side of the road, on the steps of a white farmhouse,
some other soldiers, about five of them, were sitting. Beyond
the armored car there was a large truck in the road, pointing
the other way, a circling antenna on the roof. Ring walked
slowly forward, a moment of qualm: are they stopping the
contaminated? The well-dressed officer in the immaculate

helmet was watching him come, slowly moved to attention, gave suddenly, swiftly a delightful salute. The men behind him came to attention. Ring took a deep pleasant breath. The officer said, "Mr. Ring. Good to see you. How do you feel, sir?"

Ring nodded, breathed.

"We're clearing the road, sir. Orders of General Armitage. There'll be an Emergency Team here reassembling. I'm, ah, under General Armitage's command, sir. But it's very good to see you."

Ring nodded again. He said slowly, trying to get organized, "What about the radiation? Can you detect it?"

"No, sir. Not here, sir. But we've got the area in tap right now, sir, and it's just a little way down the road, and still apparently moving slowly. This way."

"Still moving."

"Yes, sir."

"Are you going to hit it?"

"I don't know, sir."

"What are your orders?"

"To remain here until we begin to detect the approach. To remove whatever possible, whoever needs help. To find you, sir"—the officer, a Captain, smiled—"to withdraw if necessary, when necessary. To allow no one to enter. Sir, how do you feel?"

"Tired, man, tired." Ring moved toward the fender of the car, hiked up, sat there. He looked at his watch. More than an hour. And you're still alive. He grunted, shook his head. He said, "Are there many dead?"

"We don't know, sir, how many. But. Some came out rather sick. And some of those died before . . . we could help. Rest we sent on. Most of the men seem to have moved, beg your pardon, faster than you, sir. You're one of the last, apparently. Of course, there may be many men in there just sitting down, or dead already. But there have been very few in the last"—the Captain looked at his watch—"you are the first man in the last fifteen minutes. And the helicopters detect very little motion."

"Call for you, sir." Another officer, in the ear of the Captain. The Captain excused himself. Ring sat there, reassembling. He'd come at least . . . five miles. A soldier was near him. Ring asked for something to drink. The soldier went off, came back with a cup of coffee. Ring drank it. The sky was clearing. Sunlight. But . . . late in the afternoon. *"Still alive, sir."* He shook his head. The Captain came back.

"Word from the air, sir. The radiation appears to have stabilized."

"Stabilized?"

"It doesn't seem to be moving, sir."

Ring rubbed his cheek, trying to think. The Captain said, "We've got some people who fly along the edge, sir, part of the Emergency Team. They go until they detect it and then come immediately out. When they've done it a few times, then we change the men. So they've got the thing pretty well under inspection, sir. It's . . . a perfect circle, sir. So the wind doesn't seem to affect it. It just . . . apparently got a bit larger. But it seems to have stopped. Of course, no way of knowing what will happen."

"Thank you," Ring said. He drank the coffee. "Where's Armitage?"

"The General is up the road a way, sir, trying to organize mobile equipment, radios. We need some sort of headquarters, sir. He's only a short way away. But . . . we have nothing left to drive you in, sir, except this vehicle, which I've been ordered to maintain here until radiation advances in this direction. I . . . have already sent word to the General, sir, to tell him you were here, but I couldn't contact him personally. Very sorry. Must say, though, I'm glad I was able to recognize you."

"Good thing," Ring said absently.

The Captain said, "You don't remember me, sir, but I served under your command some years ago."

Ring didn't remember. He focused on the Captain's face. Vaguely familiar. A competent face, careful watchful eyes. Spoke very well. But Ring could not think. He needed a rest. He said to the Captain, "Excuse me, son. I'll just sit here for a bit."

"Yes. Ah, only one other report. There's some bad weather on the way."

"More rain."

"Yes, sir. And some wind. A front coming. We're trying to find . . . it's going to be rather difficult to reassemble the division, sir. But General Armitage is doing his best, sir."

Ring heard an engine; saw a staff car come down the road. The Captain said, "Ah. I think that'll be for you, sir."

A gray car swung to a stop. The driver did not leave, kept the engine running, waved. The Captain nodded.

"That's for you, Mr. Ring. General Armitage sends a staff car."

Ring slowly walked forward, hands in pockets. The door of the car popped open. Driver was . . . a sergeant. Ring nodded. The Captain was following him. Ring turned.

"What's your name, Captain?"

"O'Brien, sir."

"Take care," Ring said. He put out a hand. The Captain shook it. Ring thought: any moment now, the thing could come again. Then he thought: Richard, take care of *yourself.* Calmly, now.

The car drove off down the empty road. It was growing dark. The night was coming. But he began to wake up. It was almost as if, coming near death, you felt increasingly sleepy. But now that death was not close . . . he was waking up.

Armitage was forming a new headquarters in a new

building complex area that had many new houses with no people in them. Some of them had been there that afternoon, but there was no one there now and there were several nice new empty houses with a park nearby, and the park had a broad golf course onto which flocks of helicopters were coming. New vehicles were beginning to assemble at a wide crossroads and there were new troops moving in and worn tired troops assembling and it was very busy. Armitage met Ring with an unexpected hug: he put his arms around Ring, grinning delightedly—a happy man. He was thin and tall and scrawny and excited and delighted. Ring had long known him. He was the kind of neurotic who is nervous in peacetime and happy at war: he needed stress; he was more comfortable. He was delighted to see Ring looking so well. He had found Corelli, too, and Corelli was, *hee*, resting. Did Ring need a rest? Ring shook his head. Armitage was briefly embarrassed.

"The damned road was blocked coming out. What the hell could we do but run? Once the road was blocked you couldn't get through those trees with trucks, so you had to go by foot, but by God, we won't do *that* again. I promise you, we'll be ready now. But the thing isn't moving. Hasn't moved in quite awhile. The thing. Hee."

He looked at Ring. His face began to twitch. Ring was slowly, steadily, beginning to laugh. The "thing." Yes indeed. For a moment there the thing was very funny. Real but ludicrous, incredible, silly, impossible. Ring guffawed. Then after a while he sobered.

"Got some Scotch?"

"Can find some. But not much."

"Just a bit."

"Lots of work to do. Oh. You've got to call Hiller."

"Have you called Tesla?"

"We just got started."

"Any answer?"

"Nope."

"Damn. I hope . . ."

"Yep. *Wow!* I got to move. I'm assembling the links again. I'll let you know the picture as soon as there is one."

Ring drank the Scotch, stood on a screen porch watching troops move light armored cars into position. But it was not really a war. How do you fight an invisible moving Wall?

Ring drank more Scotch. A vacant universe. A cooling world.

Armitage assigned him a new group of aides. At least one of the others had not survived. One had come out slowly but was rather sick. Ring did not want to remember names. The aide brought in a new radio set: Hiller was waiting. Hiller was very glad to be able to talk to him. Ring explained it all slowly. Hiller did nothing but swear. Ring said, at last, "You know more than I do."

"We're putting it together. Getting the whole picture."

"What is the picture?"

"Well, the thing there suddenly got bigger. It grew. Like a damned flower. It spread out wider. The circle got bigger, but it's still a perfect circle. About fifty-five miles in radius. It spread for only a few minutes, slowly. Then it stopped spreading. It seems to be the same type of, ah, radioactivity. So, to get to the heart of the goddamn matter! the thing got stronger."

"Any idea why?"

"Nobody has a goddamn *fact.*"

"What do you think?"

"What do *you* think? You're closer to the goddamn thing."

"I don't know. I . . . all I did was run. Haven't had time to think."

"Simplest conclusion: there's a gadget in there that sends out the beams. Like a fountain. And somebody turned up the power. That seems to be what happened. Well, what do you think?"

"Possible."

"We could've hit it. We've . . . zeroed in. If it's only a machine, and we blow that town . . ."

Ring put a hand to his eyes. Throw a bomb at an invisible Wall. His brain was not clear, not at all. Hiller said, "If the thing begins to move again, I don't think there's a choice. We'll just have to hit it."

"Well," Ring said. After a moment he said, "That kid is in there. With a girl."

"He's still alive?"

"I don't even know that."

"I heard about the girl. Jesus! Alive after *five days in there*. In a goddamn cell. Well, nothing from the kid."

"No contact. We ran away and, of course, some time passed. I haven't heard anything. But we're trying now."

"Frankly, to be goddamn blunt, I don't think one kid is going to make much difference now. I think there's some gadget in there and somebody has turned the thing on, and that's the only reason, in my simple brain, why the damn thing got bigger. Somebody is conducting a goddamned experiment. You know how many died this time?"

"No."

"I don't know either. But we lost quite a few. Well, all right. Contact that kid. If you can. We'll delay for the time being. He may find something. If the thing doesn't move. But also, we're going to get in some of that automatic electronic gadgetry and back him up. I think he may need some firepower. But, advise that kid that's staying in that town, we may have to hit it. Tell him at least to be prepared. To find some cover."

"I've got to find him. I hope he's all right."

"Well, I hope he can find *something*. I tell you, Richard,

one thing I sure as hell would like to see. I'd like to see that goddamned machine."

He hung up. Ring put down the radio. He felt his heart beating. The *Thing*. The *Wall*. He began to sense a pattern. He waited, and sat there letting the mind work. It expanded five miles, in all directions, like a blossoming flower.

A man came up to the door. Ring saw: little Corelli.

A bald weary face, an open mouth, a dirty white shirt. He sat down next to Ring. He talked about the value of still being alive. He admitted that next time he would not run that fast.

Ring said, "You think there'll be a next time?"

Corelli raised flat palms, gestured. He looked up into the dark.

"Thy will be done."

An aide popped up to the door.

"Mr. Ring."

"Yes."

"General Armitage sends his regards. Thought you might want to know this."

Ring saw lightning flare in the gray sky, remembered what the Captain had said about the coming of a storm. Ring said, "Go on."

"Well, sir, we don't follow this at all. But an airplane just went by overhead, a few minutes ago, and flew on into the Zone."

"An airplane."

"Yes, sir. Must have been a private plane. Low altitude. We had no contact on radar. We just saw the thing pass over, and we picked it up. It was a small twin. I don't know what kind. It flew right into the Zone, into the, ah, lethal area."

"An airplane."

"Yes, sir."

Ring sat there. Lightning flashed again. He could feel the

wind beginning to pick up. He said softly, "Now, why would anybody, in his right mind . . . ?"

The aide suggested: "Sir, General Armitage says that it may be just someone lost. That's the most natural conclusion. Some private pilot that doesn't listen to the media, so he doesn't know about the Zone. Always a fella like that. But the General suggests one other point. There might be someone aboard the aircraft who knows about the Zone and who knows he himself is immune to the radiation, and so he's flying in as a part of some, ah, Team."

Ring sat there. The aide said, "The General wanted you to know his thoughts, sir. We'll let you know as soon as we have anything concrete."

The aide departed. Ring sat in silence. Armitage would think of the enemy. Instantly. But the fact was . . . that the enemy is possible.

Behind the Wall . . . someone sits . . . with a machine.

Shepherd.

The name came from the back of the brain. Tesla? Nick. I hope the kid's all right.

The rain began again but it was heavy rain with much thick wind and lightning and thunder, and some of the lightning was very close and came down into the golf course nearby and struck a tree. The wind was worse, and worse, and the rain began to blow in through the screen, and Ring went inside with Corelli to a strangely carpeted room, with lights flickering because of the lightning, and he sat in the sound of thunder.

FIVE

Nick Tesla woke to the sound of rain. Hard rain blowing against the window. He could see streetlights glowing wetly on steaming windows. He went back to sleep. He was awake again before dawn and saw the girl still asleep, and he went outside and sat watching the sun rise and the roof of the world come aglow and the rain lighten, soften, and the wind die, the morning come. Pools in the streets, many, many leaves, no lights in the houses but lights on the street. He had a rare moment. Awake in a new world. The traffic lights blinked, but no one drove by. He felt an odd calm. He thought: not a bad town. Quiet. You can walk the streets.

He shook his head.

Nick, old buddy, you're a nut.

But he felt no tension now, nothing to be afraid of, not even the dogs. He was going to turn on the radio and see if anybody would talk to him about anything at all, and then he saw the girl standing by the bars, holding herself up.

"Hi," Nick said happily.

The girl stared.

"How're you doing?"

The girl nodded.

"I'll tell you, you had me worried. You sleep all right?"

The girl nodded. She was young. Wide-eyed. Pretty. Twenty? More. Honey, today, please talk.

"Be careful, sport. You might fall down. You must feel kind of weak."

She had a green blanket over her shoulders; she tugged it up to her neck. Her hair was scrambled and her eyes were puffed, but she had a lovely mouth, a pleasant nose, a graceful face. Nick said, "No fresh eggs this morning. But I've got some coffee and beans and some stale bread. How about that? You like that stuff? I can find a can outside, of almost anything. Just ask."

She said softly, "Anything."

"Um." She had spoken. Praise be. He grinned.

"Just ask me, lassie. Anything you want. I can find almost anything, honest."

"Anything," she said again. Her voice was very soft, her eyes were dark and childish and trustful. She stood holding herself erect, staring at him. He said, "How do you feel?"

"All right."

"Anything I can do? Do you have any pain?"

She shook her head.

"You must have been in there five days. My God! Five days by yourself. In that place. I don't know how you took it."

She grimaced, blinked.

"Listen," Nick said. He came forward slowly, stopped near the bars. She did not move away. He said, "You can come out now. If you want to."

She nodded. Then she said, wide-eyed, "Five days?"

"Yep."

"Was it that long?"

"Yep. Sure was."

She trembled. She said, "I don't remember . . . clearly."

"I guess not. But you look fine. Really. You'll be all right."

"Can I come out?"

"Oh, sure. You want to open the door? I have to open it. I'll do it right now. Now, be careful. Take it easy."

He went back, tossed the switch. The door clicked, moved a few inches. The girl stood there, holding herself up. Nick came back, swung the door open, thoughtfully backed away.

The girl was free. She let the blanket drop. She wore a dark green dress, rather worn. Her figure was very good. She led herself to the door, stood there. Nick kept his distance.

"Need any help?"

She shook her head. Her mouth was open, her eyes in slight shock. She didn't walk in the open; she came out around the bars, still holding herself up, then slowly collapsed. He came forward and caught her. She looked up, terrified. She said desperately, "Want to sit down."

"Okay."

She sat on the floor with her back against the bars. Her fingers were shaking. She looked about ready to cry. Nick tried to be consoling, but he was scared. He had no idea what to do, how long it would take.

"Listen, lassie, now you take it easy. You need some food, that's all, and maybe a little exercise. If you need any help, just ask. Whatever you want. Anything I can do. Though God knows, I'm not much use."

She moved her hands down, rubbing her thighs. The dress was up high and she had no hose on her legs and they were long and very nice. He turned away, started to cook, chatted about food while he heated a TV breakfast of eggs and sausage. Not much of a breakfast, but he was not much of a cook, and apologized while trying to remember when or if he had ever once cooked breakfast for anybody, certainly not for a pretty girl who had just woke up, and the thought of the new world was again rather eerie. But it was *real*. The coffee was good coffee. The lovely girl sat there and drank and ate while he sat there and chatted about the food you could get in the stores, and come to think of it, the price was right. She ate slowly and he could see that her face was stronger, her skin unwashed but healthy, pink, her eyes clear, dark, rather bright. She glanced up at him and she was looking at him, really examining him with different eyes, and there was something in the dark eyes that was rather powerful. He thought: *interesting*. Wonder how old? Doesn't look, maybe twenty? She put down her plate.

"How do you feel?" Nick asked.

"Five days," she said.

Nick nodded. "Yep."

"My mind has not"—she pursed her lips—"my mind has not been working. But . . . it seems to be working now. Is it working now?"

Nick smiled. The girl said, "I'm really . . . all right?"

"You're one of the very few. Most of the rest of them, in this town, aren't alive. I guess I'll have to explain."

He did. But as she listened her eyes went blank and she turned her head away and he shortened the explanation. When he stopped talking, she opened her eyes and looked up at him with a confusing, peculiar look and said, "Thank you."

"Hm?"

"I'd like to try to walk."

She started to get up. He had to help her, and wanted to, and held her arm. She held the bars, made it to her feet. After a moment she said, "My legs."

"Let me help you."

"I never went that long without food. You feel . . . really awkward."

He put his arm around her waist. "Come on," he said. They walked down the hall, passed a blanket-covered body. She turned her eyes away.

"I'll be all right in a minute," she said. She sat in a chair by the desk, put her head in her hands. Then she said, "How many are dead?"

"Seventy thousand." Easy to say: a simple phrase.

She sat with no expression on her face. She did not ask any more questions; he did not volunteer information. She was a girl with a troubled brain and he did not know how much of it was the five days locked in an empty jail and how much had come from before that, so he thought the only thing to do was to help her and shut up, but at the same time there was something in the look of her face, some sort of brightness in the eyes, that told him she was rather a bright girl, not only well constructed but complex in the head, and he was becoming more curious every moment, but he waited. The girl looked toward the body in the cell, looked at it, then looked away, stood up, went to the window by herself, looked out into the morning light. She gazed. Nick said nothing. After a moment she turned, held herself against the wall. She said, "One thing I'd like to have. Soon as I can. Could I take a *bath* somewhere? Get myself clean?"

She closed her eyes. Nick said, "A bath? Sure. I guess so. But I don't know . . . exactly where."

"I'm filthy." She shuddered, looking down at herself, plucked at the green dress. "I've got to wash myself."

"Well, the electricity is still on. And . . . there's got to be a shower here someplace."

"I'd like, please, a bath. A bathtub. If possible."

Nick brooded. His mind glimmered: hotel? He said, "Hey. There's a downtown motel just down the road a ways. I can drive you right there, and with the electricity still working, hey, ought to be easy to find an empty room with a good bath and towels and all that. How about that? Want to try that? Of course, there may be a few dead people."

She nodded. She put out a hand. He came and helped her walk, holding her hand only: she gripped him and walked to the door; she shuddered.

"I hope you don't mind the smell of *me*," she said.

"Uh, no," Nick said honestly. "I don't smell a thing. Really."

She stood in the open door, staring up the wet, leafy, empty street. Nick thought: no dogs? Where? Watch it. She said, "I'm sorry about this dress." She was apologizing.

113

Nick said quickly, "Hell, no matter. Want to get another one? Nothing to it. We just hop down the street and go right on in a woman's place. There's one right down there, one over in the Mall. No problem. Pick whatever you want. And no charge. Hm."

He grinned. The girl looked at him. There was a sudden flush of warmth on her face, warmth in her eyes. Nick said, "There's my car. Let's go down the steps. Here. All right?"

He walked her down. She was better now: wobbly but not dizzy. He opened the door. She got into the front seat, sat next to the rifle. He got around to the other side, still looking for dogs, and was apologizing for the rifle when she reached out and touched his forearm, light coming out of her eyes.

"Bless you," she said.

"Um?"

"You are a saint. Even if you are real. And this isn't a dream."

"Saint?"

"Are you real? Are you really there?"

"I think so," Nick grinned.

"Really?"

"Yep. Saint Nick. That's me. Only . . . wrong time of year."

"Your name is Nick."

"Yep."

"Well, thank you, Nick."

"Um. Well, what's your name?"

"My . . . name . . . Ruth."

"Well. Good morning, Ruth. Now, let's go take a bath. Um. Excuse me. I mean, let's *you* take a bath. How do you feel?"

"Better. Much better. Thank you."

He went around to the driver's side of the car. They drove down the main street and he pointed to a dress shop he knew and she asked to stop, and so they went right in, breaking right through a glass door with a rifle barrel. He heard a burglar alarm. It went on ringing, rattling. He stayed outside looking for dogs but there were no dogs at all, and he stood there happily in the growing light feeling incredible and unique and strangely marvelous while the girl walked in by herself and found a dress, a blue dress, and came out holding it across her arm. Nick said, "Don't you want anything else?"

"Well, I need other things, but . . . just a dress now."

"You can get anything later. Anything." He shook his head, amazed at the truth. All the doors were open. "Amazing," Nick said.

"I wish I had something to wear—under this."

"Well, just look around."

"But I want the bath first."

"Okay, whatever you want. There's the motel. See? That one. Do you know that one?"

She shook her head.

"This isn't my town," she said.

"Well, I've tried that one, and it's not bad. Got some good bathtubs. If the electricity is working. Which with all the lights on . . ."

He checked the keys in the motel office, which was —thank God—empty, and some keys were missing, so he assumed that would be where the dead people were. He took a few keys to check and found an empty room, a room without a smell, and checked the lights and hot water and naturally they worked. He said, "Power plant must work by itself. I hope it holds up for a while longer. But . . . you can always get a generator. Um. Well, okay. All right? I'll just . . . wait outside."

She came with him to the door, touched his arm.

"You'll be all right alone?" Nick said.

"Yes. I think so now. If not, I'll call you."

"Fine."

She stood for a moment by the door, looking past him into the silent, sunny town.

"It's so still," she said softly. "So empty." She put a hand to her throat. "This isn't a"—she couldn't finish.

"Nope."

"I mean, no one here. No one here at all. But you and I. This isn't a dream."

"Uh-uh." He shook his head, smiling.

"But it's so *beautiful*."

"Beautiful?"

"Don't you think so?"

"Well." He thought: beautiful?

"You'll wait for me? Right here? You won't go away?"

"I'll be right here."

"Thank you." She reached out, touched his hand. "I won't be long."

She went into the room and stood in the door looking out again, watching him to make sure he did not go, waved to him, then closed the door.

He went out on the steps and sat in the sunlight, watching for dogs. Beautiful? Well, in a way—without the dogs. It's very quiet, and empty . . . and free . . . really *free* . . . well, now the girl, she's beautiful. Lovely face. But the legs especially. Long, long legs, like a ballet dancer's. Um. Well . . . the radios. Call somebody? Yes. From the car, see if there's . . .

He saw something move in the corner of his eye, looked up . . . there was a man with a rifle standing on the roof of a building, a high bank building, down the street.

The man just stood there, rifle hooked under his arm, looking down at Nick. The rifle wasn't aiming.

Nick sat, mouth open. The man seemed to be watching him. The man was . . . fifty yards away. Nick stood up. The man backed away, was suddenly out of sight. Nick said loudly, "Hey. What the hell!"

At that moment a car came around the corner.

It was the aged black Ford.

It came forward slowly through clumps of wet leaves, then swung to the curb near Nick, came to a stop.

There was a man inside with white hair.

He came out of the car. Nick without knowing it had pulled the .357 from his pocket. The man coming out of the car was a little man, round, rather old. Very old. He smiled, waved, said, "Good morning. How are you? Good to see you."

Nick recognized him. He was the old composer. He taught at the University. Name was . . . Hungarian. Nick didn't remember the name. Nick stood there, pistol in his hand. The old man came up, hand out, blinked at the pistol.

"Good to carry that, yes, I know, I've seen them. Well, how are you? I think I recognize your face. They have had your face on television. You are the young man who has come in for the government? Am I correct?"

Nick nodded, shook the old man's hand. It was a strong hand. The old man gave his name. It was complicated. Nick gave his own. The old man seemed genuinely delighted.

"So *very* good to see you," the old man said happily, grinning. "I've seen so far, oh, you are the twelfth person I've seen alive. Twelve of you. And me. Walking in a dead town."

The old man had a round face and a short beard and much wild white hair flowing around on top of his head and a big mouth with a big grin. He reached out, patted Nick on the arm.

"My God, but we are lucky. I do not understand, not for one moment. One thinks, at night, of the will of God. Ha." The old man bobbed his shaking hair, grinned. "Well, how do you feel? You look fine. But how do you feel about all the dead?" The old man was intently watching Nick's face.

Nick said, "Well, you don't see many."

"That's true." The old man nodded, cocked his head to one side. "But there are very very many. Yes. But I was afraid at the beginning, and so waited to die, and once I even prayed. But I did not die. And now"—the old man shook the wavy head—"well, now I just enjoy myself. I just wander and look at things, and find people and talk, which is very pleasant, and then I go home and watch television and play my piano. Ah, excuse me. I talk too much. But, how are you getting along?"

"Okay." Nick put the .357 in his pocket.

"Have you learned anything, about the cause of this?"

"No. What do you know?"

"Nothing at all. It is, ha"—the old man puffed his lips—"you and me, perhaps we are a choice."

"Listen. A few minutes ago I saw a man over there, on that roof." Nick pointed. "He had a rifle in his arms."

The old man nodded, looked, saw nothing, waited. But he did not seem surprised. Nick said, "Well, how many of those are there?"

"All of us carry a gun now. I think someone may have been killed by the dogs. They've formed packs, you know. But—on that roof?" The old man squinted. "My eyesight is poor. But . . . everyone I see now has a gun. You have that thing there in your pocket."

"But have you seen anybody shoot at anybody?"

"No." The old man stared at him.

"You have no idea what caused all this?"

"No."

"You haven't seen anything . . . questionable?"

"Have you?"

"Nope. But I've only been here . . . one night. How long have you been taking this?"

"I woke up . . . the first morning."

"You've been here since the beginning? Wandering around?"

"Yes."

"And you've seen a few people? And that's all? Listen, does anybody know *anything*?"

The old man shook his head. After a moment he said regretfully, "I'm sorry."

"Well, must say I'm curious. I wonder . . . how long it will last."

"I keep waiting," the old man said. "Mind if I sit?" He sat on the concrete steps, folded his arms, admired the sky. "I kept waiting to die. I am ready. But then, I am rather aged. So I worry less, perhaps, than others. But I do not worry very much. As long as there is light at night, and a few people every day, there is no real threat in the air. There is nothing I am afraid of."

Nick sat. He thought: a peaceful morning in an empty town sitting side by side with an elderly man in an otherwise empty world. He sat wordless. The old man said, "You were not here when this began, I know. Television spoke about you. That first morning, when I woke up, of course . . . I did not know. Not right away. I felt nothing. It was of course . . . very quiet. I had breakfast by myself. I live alone, you see, and I am somewhat happy to be in a . . . quiet place. But that morning, I began to notice, slowly, that there was much silence. Very pleasant, and I sat eating in the silence, and I went to a window, and looked out, and there were no cars on the streets, and no people. I sat there for a while, you see, not knowing anything at all, not worried about anything. But I will never forget . . . the empty street."

The old man stopped. Nick said, "Go on."

"You would like to hear?"

"Yes."

"Well, I sat there in the morning and saw no one. No cars. I turned on my morning radio. I do not turn on television in the morning." He chuckled. "I usually do not turn it on in the *evening*. But that morning, on the radio, there was

119

nothing. I tried to find some sound somewhere. But there was nothing. That was the first time I began to feel, that perhaps, but"—he hunched his round shoulders, smiled —"I did not even think of the television. I went outside and stood there, and the silence was . . . unusual. Unique." He paused, smiled again. "If you are a musician . . . you can perhaps understand *real* silence. But . . . the silence that morning . . . was new."

"Sure as hell was."

"You heard that sound. The sound of silence?"

"Yes."

"Well, then, you know. Of course. I heard . . . nothing but my own heartbeat. I went over next door. Knocked on the door. There was a woman there who is, was, a close friend. But, she did not answer the door. That was when I began to wonder. I looked at other houses. Cars had not moved from the driveways. So I did not go anywhere else. I went back into my house. I tried the telephone. There were no answers. I began to feel, perhaps, that I had gone mad. So for a while there I just sat telephoning. But no one answered. That was the bad hour."

"Did you feel like you were dreaming?"

"No. Never . . . thought of that. Other people do. I've spoken to some about this same moment. With each one I've met it's . . . different. I thought I perhaps had gone mad. So I went and got myself a good strong drink of good whiskey, and sat there drinking. And then after some time of silence I turned on the television set. And that was how I knew."

"Um. Why didn't you leave?"

"Ah, well." The old man smiled a shy smile, then chuckled. "I was slightly drunk. A little." He looked up at the sky, held a palm over his eyes. "I went on drinking a bit, and waiting, and drinking, and waiting . . . and I'm still waiting, though I"—he smiled—"no longer drink quite so much."

"Five days." Nick shook his head. "You and the girl."

"The girl?" The old man hadn't seen her.

"Oh. She's the one . . . I found her. She's in there taking a bath."

The old man smiled happily, a sudden pleasant glow.

"One more. That's very nice. I met a woman yesterday afternoon. She has a house with a large lawn down by the church over there, the big one, you know? She was sitting on a lawn at a white table having coffee with a man I'd already met, Mr., ah, Jackson. Yes. Her name is Godwin. She asked me in for coffee, and we sat on the lawn behind her lovely fence having coffee and then the rain came. But she says anyone is welcome to come to her house, since she's rather lonely and afraid of dogs, and does not shoot well, and needs some help. Do you know where the house is? Let me show you."

The door opened. Ruth came out. Nick stood up, the old man bobbed up with him. The old man was delighted.

Ruth wore the new dress: dark blue, long-sleeved, white-trimmed, a wide flowing skirt. She was drying her hair with a yellow towel. The old man gushed in a foreign language. Then he said, "Ah, but the luck of it. The luck of it to us is . . . good morning, miss."

Ruth came down, cupping the towel around her hair. She was very pretty. She looked older, calmer. Her chest was full against the dress and Nick was aware that she did not seem to be wearing anything underneath it and her body was a jolt to his eyes. The old man was saying, "It is my great pleasure to see you. I am absolutely, immeasurably, inconceivably delighted." He chuckled. "A thing as lovely as you. In this fair city. May I have your hand?"

Ruth put it forward, one hand holding her hair, and the old man kissed it, said something in detectable French, gave his name, asked hers. Ruth answered politely, a pleasant voice. She seemed stronger, in control. She no longer seemed to need help. Ruth said, "How many people are there here?"

The old man thought, chuckled. "Thirteen. I've met. Hm. The unlucky number. Well, all the rules are broken now. Every last rule is dead. Well, mademoiselle, how do you feel? Can I do something for you?"

"No, thank you. Nick, here, has been a great help."

"Well, then, I will be going. I am looking for some chickens." He waved, started toward his car. "I tried to feed some animals, some cows and chickens. But it cannot be done. They won't be kept alive. So I thought I'd get some chickens, which I did a long time ago when I was a boy, and I can fix them myself and at least have some fresh meat." He stopped, hand on his car door. "Would you like some fresh meat? Oh, and would you like some music? Let me give you my address. And perhaps you can telephone me."

He fished in his pockets, chatted away about the location of the house where Mrs. Godwin would serve coffee, came up with a paper out of a wallet with his address and telephone number on it.

"And where can you be reached?"

"I really don't know."

"Well, then. Please come by. If you are at all lonely. And I certainly hope the thing does not spread again as it did yesterday. But, on the other hand, to be perfectly, absolutely, utterly, optimistically truthful, I hope it goes on this way for a while, because it is rather pleasant." The old man touched his mouth, patted it. "There, I've said it. I shouldn't have said that. But . . ."

"Wait. It *spread* yesterday?"

The old man was getting into the car.

"Oh, yes. But . . . you didn't know that?"

"It spread out from *here*?"

"Oh. Yes. I'm sorry. I thought you knew."

"You mean there are more dead people? The thing got wider?"

"Yes."

"How much wider?"

"Only a few miles. But it is a little bigger today than yesterday. But it did not kill thousands, as it did the first time. And you and I, it did not affect us. So we go on with luck. Another day. Well, *au revoir*. If you need me at all. Or if you like chicken."

He waved, drove off. He was humming. Nick said, "Ring. My God, he could be dead."

Ruth stared at him. None of this was quite real to her yet. She was waiting for the world itself to do something. Nick said, "Excuse me. But the thing apparently got worse yesterday, and that's why I couldn't get anybody on the radio, and Jesus, they could all be dead. I'll try again. I hope he's not dead. But maybe I'll get somebody."

He went to the car, turned on the radio. It blinked, was working. No sound. He picked up the mike, pressed it, said "Hello, hello, this is Nick Tesla. Anybody there?"

In seconds, a voice came back. Unrecognizable. But excited.

"Mr. Tesla. Are you all right?"

"I'm fine. Who's that? What the hell's going on?"

SIX

The town of Jefferson had grown along the banks of a short shallow river that came out of the marshland to the northwest. It was a quiet, salty river with no mainstream: it wandered out between the mangrove swamps into the shallow Gulf. A path out to sea had been dredged through the soft bottom so that there was a course out through the swampland that boats, usually only fishing boats, would follow, and that part of the Gulf water was not popular for any boat with depth, and it was quiet and beachless and generally waveless. But it was the one thing the town possessed that had ever given Nick a sense of joy, a memory of home: the path of water leading out to the open sea. There was good fishing on the flats out in the open and mullet in the river, and far enough upstream in the freshwater area there were some good bass, and Nick had often fished both ends of it as a boy. In the last few years there had been many buildings erected along the water banks, what few there were, and a large marina, and then some condominiums, and so there were now many boats on the water and Nick had not been there anymore for a long while. But this day it was the place where the girl asked to go. Ruth wanted to go down to the river. Nick drove her down to the marina in his car. He told Ring to wait a minute; he would leave the kid here while he went off to check the school. So he parked by the marina, and they got out together by a long row of boats.

Nick said, "Now, what are you going to do? You've got to be careful."

"I'll just—find someplace to sit down."

Nick looked down the silent row. No motion. Low tide. Any dead bodies aboard? Must be some. He had not been there a long time, and he did not recognize any of the boats, some of which were big and new. A strange sensation: to stand there by a silent river watching silent boats in the silent morning. And yet . . . no danger. He heard a flip-flop: a mullet had hopped out in the river . . . which was empty. No boats moving. But there might be someone. Just one boat. He shook his head, feeling jittery. For whom doth the bell toll, old boy?

Ruth was walking. He followed her, thinking again of the damned dogs. Get her aboard a boat. He saw: down at the end of the dock, by the gas pumps, a long white boat, brand-new fiberglass, one of the longest he'd ever seen here, with a flying bridge. At least forty feet. A diesel? Rich man? Where would he be?

Ruth was walking down the dock toward the end of it, toward the white boat. The river was really empty. Again a leaping mullet, downstream. No smoke upriver. Up there was the paper plant and usually it smoked badly, and sometimes when the wind was wrong it clouded the area like white fog. But no smoke today. Nick held the rifle in his hand; the .357 was lugged in his pocket. He thought: give her one? But she will be safe on a boat. He watched her legs move as she walked. She stopped by the north rail, looked out across the river. Nick said, "I want you to take care of yourself. Why don't you get aboard something? Better look and see if you can find something big and empty, maybe that big one there."

He pointed at the white flying bridge. The girl looked, nodded, walked that way. Nick thought: hope there's no dead stuff aboard. Well, you can always move it out. Dead bodies. Haven't thought of that.

Could you?

He stopped, tried to picture it.

Sooner or later, survivor, you'll probably have to . . . carry the dead.

The girl opened the railing gate, stepped aboard the white boat. Nick thought: she doesn't talk much. He stepped on the boat. Who owns it? The back of his mind said: it no longer matters.

The girl went to the rear railing of the boat, stood silently looking out across the flat dark water. Nick went by the controls, opened the door going down, took his time, took a breath, looked.

Empty.

No dead bodies.

There was a dining center and the kitchen in the middle, and a bedroom forward and one aft, and twin diesels. All very neat, tidy, empty. The owner was gone. Had not returned. If he was alive, he would have returned. Well. Perhaps not. Nick came back out into the sunlight. The girl seemed preoccupied. Nick found an aluminum chair, portable, bendable; he opened it, she sat.

He began to think: would be nice to go into the river in this.

Can take it out anytime if I want to.

Nobody out there.

My boat.

Free country.

No man is an island.

"Hm."

The girl gave him a sudden smile. She reached out, touched his arm.

"Thank you."

"Well, I ought to go. There's . . . nobody down below. They've got a kitchen, so if you need something."

The girl nodded. But she looked back toward the flat marsh downstream. She said, "It's so *empty*."

"Yep. Does that bother you?"

"Not at all."

"Really?"

"I'll be fine here."

"Well, if you need something from the stove down there, I can show you how to work it."

"I know how. Thank you."

"Well, I guess I ought to go."

"Will you be long?"

"I don't know. I guess, an hour or so, at least."

"I'll wait for you. Can I make lunch for you?"

"Oh, sure. I'll appreciate that. Can you cook?"

She smiled again, really radiant, startling. "I *love* to cook," she said. White clean teeth, straight and strong and neat. Very, very pretty girl. "What would you like? I can pick it up in the Mall. But it will all be in cans."

"Be careful. Listen, you better not do that until I get back. All right? I'll take you in the car. We'll go together. I won't be that long. Okay? Stay here?"

"All right."

She smiled that blossoming smile. He felt his chest thump. He waved, bobbed his head, went through the gate and down onto the dock. He turned, waved again. She nodded, sitting calmly, regally, legs crossed and the dress far above her knees, and Nick wandered back toward the car. He got into the thing feeling rather fine. No man is an island. Later on, by God, why not take that boat out and take it downriver and take it outside, and maybe fish a little? Why not?

Wilco.

Roger.

He chuckled, drove toward the University.

That town was suddenly somewhat pleasant. For a long moment he did not miss anything or anyone or think at all about dead bodies. Then he drove past an office building where he had gone the month before to an ancient dentist called Old Harry, Old Harry Maguire, and Nick looked up at the office remembering the life that had been there, and wondered if Old Harry had made it, was Old Harry alive? No way of knowing. But . . . he doubted it. For whom the bell tolled. A moment later he passed the lawn behind the steel fence and saw a couple sitting out near a small white table, sipping coffee: the couple the composer had told him about. They waved at him. He waved back. He almost stopped, thought—*later*—and drove toward the school.

Incredible.

You don't *see* anybody dead.

Remember, in all the houses . . . they lie.

Thank God you don't see them. Dead baby.

He went through the gate that led in to University grounds and down the long road between the dogwood trees. No cars anywhere. Not even a bird. He parked along the edge of the green between the library and the physics building. He told Ring where he was going and took the hand radio and the rifle and started to walk across the green toward the physics building. The sun was bright and warm, and the wind, which had been still, was picking up. He saw leaves moving across the green, and then a voice said, "Mr. Tesla."

A loudspeaker.

He stopped. The voice was metallic, from the right side of the green, very loud.

"Mr. Tesla. You are on private ground."

To the right. Atop the library. He stared. Searching. The voice said, "Mr. Tesla, this is private ground. You are not allowed here."

131

He stood there. The voice was steady, even, metal, inhuman. The voice said, "You are not allowed upon this ground. You will immediately withdraw. Mr. Tesla, you will withdraw."

Silence. Nick stood there, looking. He saw no loud-speaker. He looked right and left—no motion.

A bullet struck the ground in front of him: dirt popped. He heard the blast to the right.

He dropped the radio, crouched, bringing up the rifle.

A bullet flicked the ground to his right. Bits of dirt and grass splattered against his pants. He was in the open, in the wide open, looked, could see nothing. He began backing, searching, holding the rifle.

Another bullet drove into the ground in front of him, spattering dirt against him. He thought: *run*. He did.

He turned and went toward the trees as fast as possible. Even while running and expecting every second a bullet numbing into his back he was thinking: they didn't hit me. Bad shot? No. I was wide open, motionless. They didn't hit me. Didn't want to hit me. Safe. Don't worry. But he ran as fast as he could into the trees and hunched down behind a small dogwood, holding the rifle, remembering finally to load the damned thing, but no other bullet came, and he stood there for a moment, not knowing what to expect, not knowing whether to fight back or how or against whom, waiting for another shot, but nothing else came. His car was there. He went over and got in and sat there, but there was nothing to do but get the hell out. He drove off. After a moment he turned on the car radio and told Ring what had happened. Then he went back to the boat, but Ruth wasn't there.

* * *

Ring and Armitage were listening together. They heard the sound of the voice from the loudspeaker but it was too faint for them to hear what was said. Then they heard the thump of Nick's radio striking the ground. They sat for some moments in silence, waiting. Ring heard what he thought was gunfire. He began to see the young man in his mind: lying on green grass with blood coming out of him. He sat there. He looked at Armitage finally, and was beginning to swear when Nick's voice came on and Nick explained what had happened, and in the background he could hear the sound of the engine of Nick's car, and Ring felt a flood of cool, blessed relief, along with a rising anger at his own helplessness. He said, "You couldn't tell how many?"

Nick said, "I couldn't tell anything. Goddamn, I dropped that little radio."

"Well, you've got another in the trunk, a backup if necessary. But what do you think: they *weren't* trying to kill you?"

"I don't think so. Hell, I don't know. All the bullets were close. But they didn't fire when I ran. And they were close enough. If they really wanted me *dead*, I think I'd be dead. I think they were just warning me, driving me away. Hell, I don't know."

Ring said to Armitage, "What can we send in to help him?"

Armitage swore, shook his head.

"Where's the equipment?" Ring asked. Then he understood. All the mobile units were left behind when they ran. All the backup material was now inside the Zone, behind the Wall. Ring said, "We can send him some stuff. We can send him a tank. Yes. He can get inside and be safe from anything they have, anything, and he can blow hell out of anything."

Armitage said, "It'll take time."

"How long?"

"All day. It's being flown in. I'll have to . . . I really *am* sorry. I'll have to order. Be here in a few hours. Exactly what do you want?"

Nick said, "I don't hear you guys."

Ring said, "We're going to send in some equipment to protect you. But it's going to take time. Do you want to come on out?"

"What kind of equipment?"

"A tank. Or rather, something electronically guided, but armed like, and looks like, a tank; you'll be safe inside there. You can fire back. We can guide it all from here. You'll have a small cannon, and a machine gun, and you'll be safe inside."

Armitage called an aide, started giving orders. Nick was silent for a moment. Then he said, "A tank. You want me to go back there and fight?"

"Well, we want you to go back there."

Pause.

". . . and look around. Just go back there. Will you do that?" Ring said.

Pause.

"Okay."

Pause.

"You know why? I'm goddamn curious."

Ring thought: and we can send a demolition unit. Yes. Full armor, full power. Yes. He turned to Armitage.

Ring said, "How long will it take?"

"Hey!" Nick said.

An alarming sound. Silence. Ring said, "What's happening?"

"There's a guy coming down this way, down the road."

Ring waited. After a long, waiting, silent, paralyzed moment he said, "What's happening?"

Nick said, "A big guy. Coming this way. Carrying a rifle. He . . . just waved at me."

"Does he look dangerous?"

Silence.

Ring said, "Hello."

Nick said, "I'm a little nervous. Got to put down the mike."

Ring sat there. Armitage was talking on the radio to someone somewhere. Ring turned, looked toward the Wall.

* * *

The car was a police cruiser. No light flashing. It stopped on the road leading into the marina. The man who came out was carrying a rifle. The door of Nick's car was open, and he sat on the seat behind it with the .357 in his hand. He leaned down behind the door, cocked the pistol. The man coming down was tall and gray-haired, thin, bony, wore a gray sweater. He waved, came in a slow walk, the rifle loose in his hand. He said a word that sounded like "hi." Nick propped the .357 on the car door, aiming. He said, "Put the rifle down."

The man stopped. He had wide dark eyes, dark eyebrows under thick, windblown, gray-white hair. He let the rifle slide woodstock to the ground, still holding the barrel. He said, in a soft voice, "I wasn't going to use this."

Nick said, "You won't. Put it down."

The man leaned the barrel against the wood railing, let it go. He smiled a rueful, patient, weary smile. "Sorry," he said.

"Who shot at me? Was it you?"

"No."

The man leaned against the railing. Nick instinctively aimed the .357 off to one side. Damn thing might go off. The gray-haired man spoke in a very soft voice but clear words, clear accent, sound almost British:

"You're Mr. Tesla, I gather. Your name is . . . Nicholas Tesla."

"How the hell do you know that?"

"Television." The man gave a slight smile. "There was a film this morning. You're . . . easy to recognize. You've been

135

here, ah, since yesterday. No problem? Fine. Glad to see that."

He had the eyes of the doctor making the diagnosis. Professional smile, watching, studying. Nick knew: no threat. He eased back the hammer of the .357. Those things could go off with no pressure at all. He blew a breath. He said, "That was chilly."

The man nodded.

"Sorry. But I want you to know this: no one tried to hurt you. They did a . . . foolish thing. But they weren't trying to kill you. They just want you to stay away. They want . . . no contact with you. None at all."

"No contact."

"You represent the government." The tall man smiled a patient smile. "I hope you understand this, Mr. Tesla. At this moment there's some research going on over there that's very dangerous, and very private, and we need some time. We need to be left alone. I'm sorry about that shooting. I wouldn't have done that myself, but . . ."

A car came around the same corner; another police car. Nick crouched. The car stopped, door opened, beautiful face: Ruth. Nick sagged. Ruth gave a cheery hello, came out carrying a large brown paper bag. She said hello to the gray-haired man, shielded her eyes, regarded him with delighted curiosity. "Hi. Don't I know you? I've seen your face somewhere," she said.

The man gave a polite smile. To Nick, Ruth said, "I went out to shop. Just for food. Hope you don't mind. Did I . . . worry you? Gosh. Well, I just walked over that way and saw this police car, and it had the key in it, and it started up, so I drove up to the Mall there, and it was really very nice. And oh, hey, I turned that radio on, and there were people *talking*." She was radiant. She put down the grocery bag, still talking lightly, easily, swiftly. "There were two men talking about dogs. They said that dogs were dangerous and gathering outside the town and attacking some cows, things like that, and the men had to get together to clean out dog packs. Ugh. Now I see what you mean. But I don't think . . . I would shoot a dog." She stopped, looking intently at the face of the gray-haired man. "Your face is familiar. Well, would you like something? Some coffee?"

Nick grunted. "Honey. Next time you go anywhere. In this town. Take a gun."

Ruth looked at him, back at the gray-haired man.

"I didn't see any dogs. I saw this one man. A priest." She laughed, put one hand to her hair. A happy girl. In a town filled with dead. She said, looking from face to face, "He was talking about the days of Noah, how he'd always wondered how much of that was true, and here, maybe, we go again, in the modern age. But that makes . . . how many people are still alive in this town."

The man said, "About twenty."

"That many?"

"I've met . . . about two dozen."

"Wow!" Ruth smiled. "That's amazing."

"Have you been here since the beginning?"

"Oh, yes, but . . . I stayed by myself."

The .357 in Nick's hand was down behind the door. Ruth looked back and forth. She began to sense something in Nick's face. To the gray-haired man, Nick said, "Friend, I want to know who shot, and why."

The man looked at Nick with those wide black eyes. Nick said, "Tell you something, friend. That place can be hit. Anytime. If it spreads again, it'll be blown all to hell."

"I know," the man said. He put his hands in his pockets, leaned against the railing. "Tomorrow's the seventh day."

Ruth said, "What's the matter?"

Nick felt the .357 warming in his hand. There was something . . . eerie in that man's dark eyes. Nick thought: *this is the man who knows.* The man went on looking at Nick, expressionless, thinking. Ruth backed off a step. The man held up a long arm in the gray sweater, pointed north.

"There's an army out there, Mr. Tesla, a few miles away, that wants to come in. It can't now, not yet. Not yet. But it's coming. But there's no army here now. No police, no government. It's as free right now as it will ever be again. Free. And it will stay that way. For a while. How long? I don't know. The radiation goes on. But if you live through that first day . . . you'll go on for a long time. How long? I don't know. Why? That's what I'm trying to find out. And I need some time. So I'm going to take it."

He stood up, stepped away from the railing. He looked back and forth, Nick to Ruth, sighed, shook his head. He put his hands in his pockets, blinked the dark eyes.

"One thing I know. One thing I know." He breathed a husky breath, pointed toward the school. "There's a weapon here. A new weapon. It killed seventy thousand people. It killed . . . it's very simple to make. Understand that. Please listen. That thing is easy to make. Up until now it was very difficult anywhere in the world to produce lethal radiation, nothing like that, but we've made our step, oh yes, made another step up, and now it's easy, nothing to it. Anybody can do it. So . . . if I open the gate now and the Army comes in, the government takes over, we give them a new weapon, we give it to the committees, and they'll leak, and it'll soon be all over the world . . . some governments will ban all re-search, and some will pay fortunes for it . . . oh, it will be there, it will be there. And the men who keep storing up weapons will go on storing up weapons, until somebody pushes the button. And that's the one thing I'm sure of. If the button's pushable, somebody will push it. The nature of man. God's will be done."

A long moment of silence. Sound of a mullet jumping upstream. In the far distance: crows. The man turned away, then turned back, looked into Nick's eyes.

"I suggest you leave here, son." He looked at Ruth. "Could be very dangerous. They're sitting out there ready to push their button. You know that. Well, they've been sitting there for years. But if you go on representing the government . . . and try to intrude . . . you could get hurt here, too. So. Sure, I know they can back you up. If you want them to. Point is: do you want them to?"

He reached out, gathered the barrel of the rifle, held it by the muzzle, gave a boyish, apologetic smile. "I guess I really ought to take that with me. You too, ah, Miss, sorry, didn't catch your name."

Nick said, "Wait a bit. Hold it."

The man paused, carefully holding the rifle by the tip of the barrel. Nick said, "Are you the man that turned that thing on?"

The man stood motionless for a long second. He shook his head. Then he said, "No."

Nick blew a deep breath.

"All right. What do you know about it?"

"I'll . . . tell you tomorrow. I need some time."

The man turned. Nick said, "Tell me now."

The man looked back. Nick said, "Is there a thing in there you can turn off?"

The man just stood there, motionless. Nick started to say something; the man held up a hand. The man said slowly, in that clear soft voice, "I'll tell you what I'm thinking. Look around you." The man made a slight sidewards gesture. "Look at what's left of this town. No government here now. No laws. No police. Very few people. Free. How do you feel about that?"

Nick felt a chill. The man gazed at him. The voice was cold.

"That's the whole point. May be the last point. *If the whole world were like this* . . . no more politics, no need for war . . . if we could begin all over again . . . as in the days of

139

Noah . . . but begin with the tools already here, the knowledge, the medicine, the music . . . if all the world could begin again, like this town . . . is that weapon in there a nightmare? Or is it . . . the only way out?"

The man spoke with great soft power. Nick stared at him, dazzled. The man said slowly, "Please think about that. Please do."

Nick's mind was blank, staring. The man began to walk away. Nick watched him go, motionless. The man turned.

"I'll be back tomorrow. Got work to do. Oh. I use a police car myself for the radio, as your friend did. If you want to talk to anybody, or if you need anybody, go ahead and call. Probably somebody listening. Well . . . young lady, please carry a gun when you go out on the streets. You can pick one up downtown. Well, see you tomorrow. Good-bye."

They stood silently watching him go. He drove off. After a moment Ruth said, "Shepherd."

Nick turned. Ruth was pointing at the distance.

"I'll bet you. That was Shepherd. I've seen that face."

"Who?"

"Is there really a whole army out there? Waiting to come in?"

*   *   *

Ring brought Corelli to the radio. He asked questions: height, hair color, age? He was looking at Ring, wide-eyed, hand over his mouth, astounded.

"That's him."

Ring said, "The genetics man?"

"Has to be. A. M. Shepherd. Must be. Jesus." Corelli kept his hand over his mouth. After a moment Ring said, "If *he* knows what caused the thing . . . and he's still alive . . ."

No one said anything. Then Ring said, into the radio, to Nick, "It was a *friend* of his who shot at you."

"Yep. I think so."

"So there's some kind of team."

140

"I . . . maybe."

Armitage held up a hand, pointed at the radio. Ring shut off the mike. Armitage said, "That plane that went over last night."

"What?"

"Remember the plane that went over last night? Well, could it be that somebody came in to join Shepherd? Somebody who knew what caused it, and knew *he'd* live?"

Ring felt an internal thump.

Corelli said, "Ask Tesla what he thinks of Shepherd. If he thinks . . ." Corelli tapped his skull. Ring asked. Nick said, "No. Not hardly."

"You're sure? Nothing fanatic? Wild-eyed? Nothing in the way he talked?"

"Nothing."

"Well. *If I could see him myself.*"

Nick said, "Listen. The man said he'd seen two dozen living people here. I've seen a few myself. Already. And they've been in here six days and they're not sick."

"Wait. He said something about . . . *opening the gate.* Is that what he said?"

"Right. Open the gate. Let the troops in. That's what he said. Let the government and the law back in. He was against that, no doubt of that."

"Do you think that means he can turn the thing off?"

Pause. Nick said, "I think so."

"But he won't turn it off."

"No. He won't."

"For how long? Did he say for how long?"

"No. But he did say . . . we could die anytime."

"Jesus!" Corelli said.

Armitage said, "Better call Hiller." He signaled to an aide. Ring said, into the mike, "Look, Nick, you're staying calm. Good. Very good. Proud of you. But you better come out. Bring the girl with you. Come on out. It could get sticky in there. We don't want you to risk anything. We need you. Great job. Listen, Shepherd has friends. And if that thing spreads, we'll have to hit it. You know that. So come on out. You can go back in, in the morning."

Silence.

After a moment Ring said, "Nick?"

Pause. Armitage looked at Ring with a tense, twitching mouth. Ring said, "Nick, we have a plan for you. We have a way you can hit them. We can cover you, and you can go back to that school. But we've got to get some things ready. You willing to go back?"

Nick said, "To the school? Where they shot at me?"

"Yes. But you'll have cover. We can put you inside something metallic, can't describe it here, but you'll be safe. And then you can go back. Are you willing to try that? To see what's really there?"

"Hell, yes."

"Then come on out."

"You know what? I'm curious."

"Good. We'll be waiting for you."

"Wait a minute."

Armitage was slightly shaking his head, put his finger to his lips. He whispered, "Don't tell them what's coming. Shepherd's friends may be listening."

"Hell," Ring said. He waited. Nick's voice: "Listen, the girl won't come out."

"She what?"

"She wants to stay here. I . . . can't blame her."

"It's damned dangerous in there, son."

Pause.

Nick said, "I don't really think so."

"Even the radiation, even *that*. What the hell."

"Listen, I think I'll stay."

Ring sat open-mouthed. Armitage shook his head.

Nick said, "I'm not worried. I don't think they'll do anything. The man said, he'll be back tomorrow. I'll wait for him. But I don't want to leave the girl."

Ring swore silently. Nick said, "Listen, the girl lived through six days. Nothing wrong. The man lived six days. They all do."

Ring said, "It might end at any moment."

"You may be right."

"Come on out, kid."

Silence. Armitage said, "He won't."

Nick said, "Listen, we're going to take the boat out on the river. Take a run out to the sea. We'll be away from the heart of town anyway. So, no problem. I'll stay here."

Ring had long been in command and had long given the orders and he started to give one now, but the mind balked, the mind froze, the mind stopped him: self-control. No order now. Nick was no soldier. Ring said, "Well, take the radio with you."

"Okay. Hey, one thing. Ruth says this guy won the Nobel. That true?"

"Yes."

"He did? What for?"

"Genetics."

"Genetics?"

"Yes."

"What does that mean?"

"We don't yet know."

"Hm. Well, let me know when you find out."

"Listen, boy. Listen carefully. If the thing spreads again, as it did yesterday, we'll blow that town to hell and gone. You understand that?"

"Yep."

"So come on out."

"No."

"Goddamn, I've done the best I can."

143

Nick said, "Take it easy, old buddy. Keep in touch."

"We'll keep in touch. Call me. At . . . name a definite hour. Anytime. Anything we can do?"

Nick signed off. Armitage said, when the mike was closed, "If you talk on the radio, Shepherd can be listening."

Ring put a hand to his eyes. Had not thought of that. Armitage said, "He knew who Nick was."

"That was on TV."

"Yes. But let's talk no more about the military vehicle on the radio. Shepherd has enough experience to know where to tune in. And if that kid doesn't come out, we can't tell him everything we're doing on the radio. Shepherd has friends. Hell . . ."

"I'll talk to Hiller."

"Right. But . . . we won't be ready to move today. It'll have to be tomorrow."

"No hurry. But, let's talk to Hiller, and then make the plan this afternoon. Use everything available. Get in there. Clean it up. If at all possible, *take* Shepherd. I hope we don't have to . . ."

"Can you trust the kid?"

Ring thought. He said slowly, "I'm not sure."

Corelli was sitting, plucking at his lips. Ring said, "What do you think?"

Corelli stared, white-faced.

"Did Shepherd turn that thing on in there?"

Corelli blinked. His eyes were amazed.

"Listen. Everything you can get on Shepherd, everything, get it now. Fast. *Now.*"

Corelli did not move. He said slowly, "I know . . . something."

"What? What? For Chrissake."

"I don't think Shepherd . . . would do a thing like that. He wouldn't . . . he wouldn't lie. Not Shepherd."

"Jesus." Ring pointed toward the Wall. "But he has friends there, Corelli. Friends. Where the hell did they come from? Listen, there's a *team* in there. Were they there from the beginning? Was the whole thing planned? From the beginning? Is this some . . . new kind of guerrilla warfare?"

"He wouldn't join a team. Not Shepherd."

"What are you saying? What do you know?"

"I knew Shepherd. He was no . . . guerrilla. And a man like that would never join any team."

"Then . . . all right, all right. What the hell's going on in there? Listen, is it Shepherd who knows how . . . to make a man immune to radiation? Could he have invented something that . . . ?"

"No." Corelli rubbed his forehead. "No way to do that."

"Why not?"

"Just not possible to . . . well, I don't . . . no can't be. If there's any change like that, it would have to be an adaptive trait. Yes. *That's* possible. But there's no kind of . . . *screen* . . ."

"How the hell can you be sure? It may be . . ."

"No. Look at Nick Tesla. He never knew Shepherd. Look at the rest we know. No, that's not it. Shepherd didn't invent . . . he may have found something . . . but, wait a minute, all I know is this. Shepherd was in there one day before the thing began. One day. He was visiting one of his ex-students. Man named Dave Huston. Huston was working on something genetic. In the physics area. I don't know Huston. But maybe he's still alive. Maybe *he* did it. Maybe Shepherd's just . . . protecting him."

Ring cupped hands together, took a deep breath. "Well, get Hiller. I think . . . we can hit the physics building. Just one building. We don't need anything nuclear. Fine. So. We can do it with or without Tesla. So"—he pointed to Armitage —"move, old friend." Armitage nodded, was gone. After a

moment his aide came with the hand radio and Ring told
Hiller what was happening, and Hiller, as usual, swore.
Then Hiller said, "You'll have to evacuate."

"Evacuate?"

"Wait a minute. Wait a minute."

Sunlit silence. A breeze from the south. Hiller said,
"Listen, I'm coming down there. Got to talk. Goddammit.
See you . . . tonight. Meanwhile, got to talk to that Shepherd
man. Talk on the radio frequencies. Talk any way you can,
but get in touch somehow. Order of the President. Make that
known. Okay? Fine. See you tonight."

Ring said, "Shall we plan a hit?"

"You're gonna need it."

"Who am I fighting?"

There was no answer. Hiller was gone.

SEVEN

The name of the boat was *Billy II*. An odd name for a boat, first one Nick had ever seen not named for a girl. Unless Billy was a girl. But . . . built by a woman? But after he sat aboard the boat for a while in the afternoon the idea of ownership was gone. Everything now was . . . touchable. Every boat. He sat with his feet up on the rail, and he heard the girl cooking down below: she *wanted* to cook. He was no good at that himself and he apologized for it and she said, no, happily, she wanted to do something useful, and in cooking she felt useful, and that was a new thing for her, and would he like some crabmeat? That was her specialty. He said sure, and went above, and sat there in the sunlight with a girl below with a startling figure humming down there making lunch for him. Then there was silence. Then symphonic music. Beethoven. *Pastorale.* Nick hopped down. A radio? Ruth held up a cassette player.

"I found this. It has its own batteries. This was the tape on it. Do you like it?"

"Beethoven?"

"Yes. Do you mind?"

"Not at all. I . . . like the old guy."

"It's the Sixth."

"Um."

"There's a lot more of it. The one next to it is Copland. Whoever made this liked classical music. I wonder who it was. Nobody in my family ever liked . . ."

She went back to cooking. He went back up top and sat listening to Beethoven, and then went off and plucked out the gas hose and filled the tanks. Twin diesel. He stood looking out at the empty river. Nobody out there. No one at all. Backward, turn backward, oh time in your flight . . . he tapped his temple. His head was dreamy. He wondered what the river had been like in the days of the Indians. The silence. No engines. He thought: let's go out.

They had lunch on the deck. They rigged up a lovely aluminum table and two fine chairs and had a marvelous lunch, really remarkable, and Ruth had brought a bottle of white wine—Chablis?—which she had even cooled a bit, and the lunch was delightful, and he sat there eating and watching her, and as each moment went by she was lovelier. Something gentle about the girl. Something tender. She did not want to talk. She wanted him to talk, and she did not want to think, she wanted to sit and drink wine and listen, and in the background she played the Copland music, *Appalachian Spring*, and Nick felt, you're dreaming, old boy.

But it was a superb lunch. And Ruth wouldn't even let him tidy the thing up. She said she wanted to stay busy and he wondered again why she'd been in the jail, but he didn't ask. He said, "Would you like to take a run out on the river?"

"Can we do that?"

"No reason why not."

"Oh,"—she put a hand to her throat—"I'd love to."

"We could even fish a little."

"Do you know how to work this boat?"

He chuckled.

"Yup. Trust me."

"I can go swimming out there?"

"Well, there's always a flat I can find. If you want to."

"Then let's do." She stopped, looked out over the water, shook her head. There were tears in her eyes. He said, "What's the matter? Can I help?"

150

She shook her head, reached out, touched his hand. "I'm all right. I just . . . feel very emotional."

He thought: ask her?

No.

He started the engines, investigated the gauges. Everything in order. The boat wasn't six months old. She was tied fore and aft. Ruth helped him untie: it was easy. There was a slow current going downstream, approaching low tide: this was a big boat with at least a three-foot draft so he'd have to be a bit careful at low tide out there. He swung away from the dock, gently, gently, delighted with the feel of the wheel, the power waiting there in the big quiet engines, and he moved slowly downstream, toward the markers, down a vacant river toward an empty sea.

They went all the way out. He came around the last bend and he saw the flat water, the sea against the horizon, no more land out there. He moved out into the deeper water. The girl sat in a chair by the rail; after a while she found a cloth to put around her hair, and he speeded up a bit, but never full run. He moved out into the open water and slowed, idled, drifted. A spectacular day. Perfect blue sky. A small cool wind. No boats there. Nothing anywhere. He did not remember a time when he had been out here and there were no boats at all. He cut the engines. The water was calm. They drifted slowly east. He went down below and found some fishing equipment and came up with two light spinners. Ruth shook her head, told him to go ahead. He said, "But if you want to swim, it worries me a bit. And anyway, you don't have anything to wear."

She smiled, then she laughed. She said gently, "That doesn't matter."

"You mean it doesn't matter what you wear while swimming?"

"Not really."

He grinned. "Well, it does to me."

151

He rigged a small jig, fired away: plunk. He sat on the rail.

Ruth said, "That thing with Shepherd was very interesting."

"Um. Yep. Been thinking about that."

"When I was uptown, I met this man, at the Mall, and we talked."

"Who? What about?"

"Well, he was a Jesuit. A priest." Ruth giggled. "Really. He had that white collar and I knew right away what he was, and I felt . . . very strange. I mean, to find a priest there alive in the midst of all the dead . . . standing there with *me* . . . well, you know. Well, we talked for a while. I don't remember his name. But he was very interesting, very excited. He kept going back to the days of Noah. Noah and the Ark. About those days when God decided most men were worthless and dangerous, and so God got rid of them with the Flood, all except Noah and his family. The priest kept saying he had never quite believed that, and studied the logic of it, and he was a Jesuit, and you know *them,* most of the ones I've met are pretty bright. But . . . well, it was interesting. And now out here, when you look out at the water, and the water is empty . . . I think I know what he was thinking. But . . . there's an army out there, isn't there?"

"Yep."

Nick turned toward the skyline. Great space around him. Empty world. The girl said, "So quiet."

He felt her hand on his arm. She was touching him, looking out to sea. She said, "If the whole world were like this."

He put his hand down over hers. She didn't notice. She said, "Just a few people. Everywhere. No armies. A quiet world."

Nick thought: open the gate?

A long silent moment. She looked at him. Abruptly, she

turned away, went to the rear rail, stood there looking out over the gray empty water. He cast a jig out into the silent water, quickly snagged a trout—what his Yankee father had always stubbornly called a weak fish. It was not very big, but it was pleasant to catch, the first he had caught out there in a long while, and when he asked Ruth if she wanted to cook it she said critically, no, too small, so he threw it back, and a moment later caught a charming mackerel, a charming fight, and then another, and another, and that already was enough for dinner, and they both talked about that, feeling independent, oddly comfortable, uniquely alone, and the afternoon passed quietly, beautifully. He drifted until he was close to a sandbar and then put down an anchor and told Ruth to hop in, anytime she wanted to, and he'd keep an eye out for anything dangerous, and would maybe even join her. She went below and came back up a moment later in a strange big T-shirt with a picture of a clown on the front and her legs were in blue jeans. She dived professionally into the water, swam beautifully and gracefully, rather fast. Nick watched her. After a while he decided to join her. He hadn't been out there in years and years, swimming, since the days of his father and mother. He just took off his shirt and hopped in. The pants didn't matter. The sharks did. Sharks followed the fishing boats in from the deep water, followed because the fishermen were cleaning the fish in to the water, and he had seen white sharks, and he did not like swimming out here except over clean sand. But he was happy for a while. He thought: have to take care of yourself. And if the boat doesn't start? Who do you call?

Interesting.

Swim, Noah.

He had a fine time. The girl could really move. She kept diving deep and staying underwater, and she came up in different places, with the head of a mermaid, and Nick went on feeling eerie and delighted.

153

They got out and rested, and she went down below and came back in a dress of blue brocade. It was too big for her and she thought it very funny, and then got suddenly confused, wondering how she ever had the nerve to wear somebody else's dress, and so she went below and came back in the blue dress she'd gotten that morning, and Nick started the engines—which worked well, ran smoothly, calmly, quietly, steadily—and they began the long slow path back to the town.

It was darker: the sun was going down. It went down behind a long blue cloud just above the blue water, and Nick stood by the wheel in the growing evening rounding the last bend toward the town with a gathering pressure in his chest. He felt very fine. He felt deeply confused. He aimed around the bend toward the visible marina, could see a few street-lights already glowing in the town, and he was thinking: open the gate?

Well. They'll have to open it soon.

So this can't last.

He docked the boat.

Ruth began to cook once more. She brought him coffee, and he sat on the deck in the gathering dark drinking coffee, thinking: you should get on the radio. But he didn't do that. He sat by the rail listening for the mullet, listening to music from below: Mozart now. And then the lights all went out.

The town went black.

No streetlights, no traffic lights.

There was a small glow in the western sky. A few thin clouds.

Gradually, Nick could see: the rumbled shapes of black empty buildings. It grew steadily darker: the sun was gone. He saw a light come on below and knew: we have our own generator. Ruth came up, stood near him in the dark. Nick said, "I guess the power finally failed. I guess it ran out of fuel."

Ruth said nothing. He could not see her face. He said, "Boy. Sure is different."

"It's almost . . . as if it suddenly died."

Nick felt the same thing. Ghostly dark. All the bodies. He had seen this before, power failure, but not quite like this. He felt a gathering tension. But the music came up from below. Nick felt a sudden gratitude for the boat, the presence of power. Under his feet. He remembered suddenly: airplanes at the airport. Masses of planes. He said, "We're very lucky."

"Yes. Well, I'll just go on." Ruth went back down below. Nick sat by himself.

No man is an island.

I've been an island . . . all my life.

A light came on.

Far away, in the solid dark, the square light of a distant window.

No way to tell where it was. Too dark around it. But it was the dim glow of a distant weak light in a distant window, and he knew somebody had found a lantern or a Coleman lamp or something like that, or maybe even a battery, the things you used, sometimes even candles, when the power failed. And then there was another window, far off to the right. This one coming, going, as the light moved from one room to another. This one weaker. A candle? The light there steadied in one window. The light was now stronger. Two lights in the black. And the light from below, from Ruth. Nick felt better, more relaxed, with the lights at work. He thought: what would it be like here, laddie, if you were *truly* alone?

Without Ruth. Without anybody. With no lights at all in the night.

In the dark. I would not like that.

But you're not alone.

You're just an island.

He sat watching the night rise and the stars begin to burn

in the black, great Venus first in the glowing west, wondrous evening star, clear and beacon bright. And then slowly, the moon, almost full, very clear: he could see the tiny black tints of the mountains.

There was a light on the bridge. They ate out in the night, then turned the light off and played music. They had not spoken about it, but he began to understand that they would spend the night here. Together again, as they had the night before, in the jail. To be together now was a radiant thing.

She went down, came back up with the music. This was Tchaikovsky. He had not heard it in years: something danceable. In a moment Ruth was dancing, whirling, in the dark blue dress. She moved formally, like a ballerina, her face posed and regal. She was rather good. She moved her legs winglike, spun and leaped out into moonlight. She began to hum as she danced. Then she stopped suddenly, breathless, held the rail. She said, "Oh, my. I'm really tired. You . . . have to be in shape. But I like that kind of thing. I always have."

She circled again, but she was much weaker, uneven. She stopped, put her hands to her face. He saw tears come between her fingers, but heard no sound. He started to move, didn't. She turned to the railing, faced the moon. She said, "So beautiful."

He waited. Why the jail? After a moment he said, "How do you feel about those lights out there? The window lights."

"I don't . . . it makes no difference."

"It does to me."

"Well, *you* make the difference."

"Um."

"Without you . . . I would not be here."

"Oh, well."

"I feel . . . a kind of mercy. Deliverance. Of course, I could be . . . not well. How do I seem to you? Do I seem all right?"

"Oh, sure."

"What do you think about the gate? Would you open the gate?"

"I don't know. Don't really know. How about you?"

"Not now."

He waited.

"Not for a while at least." She turned toward him. It was softly dark and he could not see the face clearly, but it was magnetic and marvelous and the back of his brain was rumbling. She said softly, "I hope you don't mind my saying that. This is your home. It's . . . not mine."

"Well," Nick said. He rubbed his face. "I don't mind being alone. Never really did. In fact, the thing I mind most, always, is the crowd. The noise. Too many people. So I guess I'm kind of spoiled by this place a little bit. But you know, I didn't expect *this*. I would have thought, in a dead town, I'd be terrified. But I'm not. It's so bloody . . . peaceful."

He remembered the bullets in the dirt that morning. But even that . . . was not a threat. Merely . . . stay away.

Ruth said, "I woke up this morning in a cell. Behind bars. And now I am here on a beautiful boat with a strong, honest man."

Strong? Honest? Nick said, "Lassie? If you don't mind. How come you were in that jail?"

Ruth turned, looked at him. Nick hastily, "If you *mind*, now."

"I don't. Not really. Not now." She came away from the rail, picked up a chair, pushed it out in the moonlight, sat down. She leaned back in the chair, propped her feet against the rail.

"I tried to get rid of myself," she said chattily, "and I was stopped late at night and locked in a cell temporarily, to be moved in the morning, only I woke in the morning after they drugged me, and when I woke up there was no one there."

"Um."

157

Ruth said, "For a while I thought I'd gone . . . insane. Really. So . . . well I may be, anyway. But . . . I just sat there and cried a bit, and waited, and slept. And nothing happened. Then I thought I was dead, and I'd gone to Hell, and this was Hell, they kept you in a jail, and didn't feed you forever, and no one ever came to see you, and you never died, all you could see was the sunlight coming in the window, but you couldn't see out the window. And I thought I was truly in Hell, and I sat down to wait, and I felt weak, and hungry, and more and more hungry, but that began to pass, and then I began to think that I might truly die, and I began to ask for that. And I became very tired. And when you came . . . I thought you were a messenger from . . . one of them."

Nick breathed, shrugged. He wanted to touch her. But he didn't move. Ruth said, "Well, let me ask you. How do I seem? Do I seem a little crazy?"

"Nothing. Nothing at all. You seem fine. Absolutely fine. Lovely. You danced like a old pro. You swim beautifully. Listen."

He stopped. Ruth said softly, "I still think of it, from moment to moment, as a dream. You're a dream. Saint Nick." She paused. He saw a dark distant smile: her hair blocked moonlight from her face. She said, "Is there anything I can do for you, Saint Nick?"

"Um." He felt heat. He wrestled. After a moment he said, "All right. Why so blue?"

She was still. He said, "If you don't want to talk . . ."

"I don't know . . . what I want to explain. I was alone." She stopped, turned back to the moonlight, looked upward, closed her eyes. She said very softly, "I was tired. I wanted to go to sleep. . . ."

He waited. He wanted the words, the reasons. So lovely a girl. What was the threat? She said, "I just didn't fit into the world. I . . . don't think I ever will. That's why this one here is so fine for me. I'm so very lucky. I'm dreaming it all, I know, but we're together in the dark, and you're Saint Nick, and I was so much alone, in a crowd."

She shook her head suddenly. "Sorry," she said. "Mustn't get overemotional. Really ought to start to think. Maybe start to cure myself. I really did want to die. But I don't now. Not now. Believe me. Don't worry. The only thing . . . as I grew older and older I found that very few people loved each other. They said it, they said it, but I began to learn that it was almost never really there. My own family. All my friends. The men I . . . I did care. I cared and cared. But nothing came back. There was nothing there. So I got finally very tired. My fault. And I just wanted to sleep. That knits up the raveled sleeve. So I lay down. And was almost gone. And have been saved, I think. Good God, what has happened today? Today, this morning, I saw the Jesuit priest."

Nick wanted to touch the girl. But he didn't move. Let her rest, in the moonlight. She was still. He did not know what to say. Be funny, lad. Sure. He said quickly, "Well, I know what you mean. Really do. I think. 'To be or not to be.' A popular speech. Always was. Always will be. 'That is the question.'"

"Have you thought of it?"

"Yep."

"Ever come close to doing it?"

"Yep."

Ruth got up, came toward him, held out her hand.

"Touch me. Hold my hand."

He held her small warm hand. She said, with a pathetic voice, "Do you think I'm . . . really all right?"

"Yep."

"You're telling the truth. Because you mustn't lie."

"I wouldn't lie."

"Because you know when somebody's crazy, really crazy, they don't even know it, they're perfectly certain that all the voices are real . . . I've seen that . . ." Her eyes were wide. Nick took both soft hands.

"Listen. I can guarantee it. It's all real. I'm sure as hell here myself. If anybody is nuts, it must be me."

She was gazing wide-eyed at his eyes. She came up and kissed him quickly, lightly, on the cheek. She went on holding both hands. She said suddenly, "I hope to God he doesn't open the gate." She looked out into the quiet dark. "Not for a while. Not for a few more days. This will be my dream world. I guess. The place you go . . . when you leave Hell."

She stepped back, turned her face away, put her hands to her hair. Over her shoulder she said, "There'll be a doctor here now, any moment now, with a shot in my arm, and I'll be awake again in a bedroom and you won't be here and I'll be in a hospital."

"Oh, hell."

"At that moment I'll wish I was dead. But now . . . is there something I can do for you?" She had her back to him. She said, "What can I do? Would you like to go to bed with me? Would that make you happy?"

She said that slowly, quietly. Nick swallowed. She turned, looked at him, nothing in her face but a mild curiosity.

"Well. Maybe it's too soon for that. Is it too soon? What do you think?"

"Well."

"Whatever you want." She just stood there, waiting. Nick finally grinned. He said slowly, "To tell the truth, I've never been asked before."

"Never?"

"Nope."

"Oh. Well . . . my life is different, of course. And I don't yet understand . . . but you saved my life. But maybe it's just too soon. Because it ought to be important. Is it important, to you? Or is it just a few moments of motion?"

"More than that," Nick said. He began to feel the strain of it. There was a sweetness in that girl, a depth in her eyes . . . he felt the blood rising. He said slowly, "I guess it's too soon."

She watched him out of the warm dark. After a moment she said, "How many people do you love?"

He took a deep breath. She said, "I don't mean girls . . . in bedrooms. I mean, really love. Like your family."

"My folks are dead."

"Are there people . . . you *really* love?"

Nick stood looking into himself in the silent dark. Eventually he said, "No."

"No one at all?"

"I have friends."

"Do you love them? How much would it hurt you to lose them?"

"Some," Nick said.

"Then you love some people?"

After a moment Nick said, "There's some people I like. But no one . . . I would really miss."

"You don't love mankind?"

He was answering very slowly, slow words to a beautiful girl in a silent night, "I guess not."

She said, "I was raised to love mankind. But I don't anymore. Not anymore. I . . . do you think many people love each other?"

"I . . . used to think so."

"What do you think now? Do you think many people love mankind?"

"Hell of a question."

"I'm sorry." She turned, stared at the moon. "I was watching television not long ago, and there was a bad, bad storm that had killed thousands and thousands of people, and I watched the pictures and felt glad I wasn't there, and nothing else, face after face, and then I felt nothing, and turned it off, and when I read a newspaper and see pictures of a wreck or a famine I feel nothing. I don't read . . ." She shook her head. "Sorry. Want to hear some music?"

She popped down and came back with a cassette: Neil Diamond. *A lesson too late for the learning. Made of sand, made of sand . . . Are you going away, with no word of farewell, will there be not a trace left behind . . . .*

They sat for a while in the gentle dark, watching the moon, not talking. Then she said abruptly that she wanted to be alone for a while and would he mind if she went and slept in the forward cabin, was that all right? And he was watchful and careful but she seemed fine and he said sure, he'd take the rear one, and she came to him and gave him the first real kiss, a flame on the lips, her arms around him, and he felt her breasts against his chest and then she left, and his brain rattled and rumbled for a moment and then he sat alone and propped his feet on the rail and gazed at the splendid moon.

He could hear a mighty silence: the flip of a moving fish, a far-off owl, the flicker of leaves in a mild soft wind. He heard music from a distance: she was playing the Beethoven Seventh. He heard the sound of an engine from far, far away, amazing how well you could hear things now from a distance, because there was no other sound, a car was moving somewhere, but he saw no light, and then one of the window lights went out: that part of town was gone in the night. He turned out the light on the deck and there was moonlight across the water and a slow flying cloud, and that one last light up the dark slope to the north, one window, a long way off. Nick thought: have to meet that person, sometime soon.

Open the gate?

He sat watching the stars, waiting for a falling star. In the dark night, with no blaze from the town. The sky was as clear as he had ever seen it here, nothing like this since a few nights long ago in the Arabian Desert near the Dead Sea.

Open the gate?

When he was a boy his father drove him in a convertible late at night in the country to show him his first falling star, and he remembered the sudden motion, the star that *moved*, and disappeared.

Open the gate?

If no one comes in, what will happen here?

His mind wandered. Roofs would fall. Trees would fall across the roads. Leaves and mud would drift and pile. But you can always get a bulldozer and clean it up. Even the airport. You can clean one strip. No more jets coming in anymore, not anymore. The dogs . . . you would thin out. You could take care of the chickens and cows . . . killing . . . money would mean nothing at all, nothing at all . . . no police anywhere . . . new and clean and quiet but not empty . . . new place . . . new way to live . . .

He sat looking up at the stars in the black silent night.

No dream.

He picked up the cold .357, held it.

A free man.

Now.

*   *   *

Midnight: Ring took a break. The demolition units had begun to arrive, and Ring went out by himself to look at them and to be alone long enough to think for a while. There were three Senators in his office with some PR men and some media people and the possible evacuation of nearby towns —Atlanta, Jacksonville—was not only an interesting subject, it was an almost impossible problem, and so Ring went off to look at the things that would blow the Wall. He had just left his office—a pleasant home with a wide screen porch—when an aide came out of the night and sprang to a saluting position: a man from Armitage. The aide said that General Armitage wanted to know what was going on in Rome.

Rome?

The aide said, "Yes, sir. General Armitage has been out in

the field and didn't hear about it until just now and if you have any time at all, sir, he'd like a few moments. If possible, sir."

"Rome."

"Yes, sir." The aide watched him eagerly.

Ring said, "What about Rome?"

The aide pursed his lips. After a moment the aide said, "Excuse me, sir, but you . . . haven't heard about Rome?"

"No."

"Oh. Beg your pardon, sir. I thought . . . the General thought . . ."

The aide made a grin, put a hand to his mouth. Ring thought: Rome, Georgia? There is a Rome, Georgia. A long way away. Ring said, "What's going on?"

"I, uh . . . perhaps you better see the General, sir, he's right . . ."

But Ring abruptly had no patience.

"What happened in Rome? What Rome do you mean?"

"Ah, well, sir, all I know is, ah, the town of Rome had an, ah, well, an *attack*. Just like the one here, sir. Just like the thing that hit Jefferson. The whole town is dead, sir. We just heard. A little while ago."

"The whole town."

"Yes, sir. Just like Jefferson."

"Rome. You mean Rome, Georgia?"

The aide opened wide his eyes.

"Oh no, sir. I mean Rome, *Italy*. At least"—the aide cupped his mouth—"I never thought of that."

"Goddamn it!" Ring said.

"No, sir. I'm pretty sure it's Rome, Italy. But if you want to check, General Armitage is . . ."

Ring turned that way. Rome, Italy. St. Peter's. Rather large city. Millions of people. Millions. Good God. The aide said something else. Ring turned. "Hiller?"

"Mr. Hiller will be here shortly, sir. He's coming in to the General's HQ. Should be here at any moment, sir."

Ring began to walk. Then he stopped. He said, "How many dead?"

"I . . . sorry, sir, I don't know."

"How wide was it?"

"Well, sir,"—the aide paled, waved his hands—"all I know is they say it's the same thing that hit Jefferson. That's all I know."

Ring thought, population: three million? More? St. Peter's. And then, from the working memory, the back of the brain: *Shepherd.* Came to Jefferson . . . from *Rome.*

Ring's brain was momentarily paralyzed, like a sleeping leg. He walked toward the light of Armitage's HQ. The back of the brain went on working. He looked at his watch: 12:18. In Rome now . . . about six in the morning. So it happened there in the early morning. Did it go on for fifty miles? Because if it went for fifty miles . . . it went out to sea.

He came up to the HQ and saw Hiller. The round man from Washington was coming up out of the dark amid a flock of aides and uniformed men. He was swearing. He saw Ring, came with a fat groping hand, puffed eyes vague behind thick lenses: a slow-moving man who talked quickly but moved slowly, was thorough, methodical, did not understand people, loved to swear, knew how to swear in foreign languages, and enjoyed it. He moved past Ring up the steps in to the HQ, a broad fireplaced room with a communications office in the dining room next to it, and Hiller said loudly, waving fat hands, "Just the hardtops, that's all. Ring, Armitage. That Corelli fella. That's all. Close the farshlugin door."

Hiller had a case filled with papers and a thick envelope, and he opened the case and slammed envelopes on the coffee table.

"Goddammit, have you talked to *him*? Shepherd? Anybody get through?"

Armitage said, "No."

"Well, goddammit, we're going to. We sure as hell better, goddamn soon. Or that town *goes*." The last word was loud. "Now, what's the setup? When can you hit?"

Armitage said, "Just about ready. Two, three hours."

"All right. We'll wait till daylight. Keep trying to talk to him. Are you trying?"

"Yes sir. But he doesn't answer. I don't think . . ."

"What don't you think?"

"I don't think he will. Because he must know that we want to talk to him. But I . . . haven't heard anything."

"Never let up, never let up."

"I've got four teams on simultaneously, all changing specified channels. If Shepherd hears anything at all, he'll hear us. But . . . we did get some answers."

Hiller said, "Who? Any names?"

"Yes, sir. I'll get you the names. But what happened . . . one of my boys was on a police frequency, and he got an answer from a man in Jefferson telling him to get off the frequency, that he was trying to talk. The man in Jefferson said he was staying in there and was perfectly all right and he wanted us to leave the line free for him to use to talk to other people in that town. We told him we wanted to talk to Shepherd and his answer, ah"—Armitage closed his eyes—"his answer was that Shepherd was the scientist, right? And my man agreed, and the man on the other end, whose name was, ah, Harrison, said he'd tell Shepherd if he saw him, but in the meantime, please get off the line. And my man said we'd keep that line open just to hear from him, and did no more talking."

Hiller said, "How long ago was that?"

Armitage, glancing at his watch, said, "Ah, about twenty-five minutes ago, sir."

Ring hadn't known about that. He had been on the evacuation system. He sat and lighted a cigarette, calmly, calmly.

Hiller said, "You've heard about Rome."

Armitage nodded, looked at Ring. Ring shrugged. Hiller said violently, "Goddammit, Richard, we've *got* to . . ."

Ring said, "Got to what?"

Hiller said, "Son of a bitch if I know." He flopped down on a couch, flipped his feet up on a coffee table. He waved his hands. "What the hell can we do? You can't bomb Rome. No way. Three hundred million Catholics. If you hit St. Peter's? Jesus!"

Armitage said, "The *whole town* is dead? All of it?"

"No word from inside. But"—he looked up with a sour smile—"we know a bit more. We were moving in on some people in that town. We had a team in there which had already, ah, arrested people, and were moving in on some others, and then it got to be late at night, and then it got very quiet, and then goddammit, it got real quiet, and nobody answered anything. So we began to know. Before anybody did. But there was nothing we could do. Right now, all Europe . . . but our team in Rome doesn't answer. Along with three million other people. And you know what? I don't think it ever will."

A moment of silence. Ring said, "What was the team doing in Rome?"

Hiller squinted. "We had our suspicions."

Ring said slowly, "What's going on?"

Hiller said, "I wish to Christ I knew."

Ring said, "Time to talk. What were you doing in Rome?"

Ring was on the edge. He had never been there before, but he was there now. Hiller looked, Hiller knew. Hiller said, "Goddamn, man, you know how it goes. We have teams. Teams that work on different things. They don't tell each other what they know. We keep it separate, goddammit, because we can't afford to share the information. Because if one guy gets caught—and one guy *always* gets caught, or quits—and he knows too much, he can sure hurt you. So. We have special teams, but nobody puts it all together. Until too goddamn late."

"You're putting it together," Ring said.

"All right, all right. Best I can. Here it is. First: we keep people checking in on scientists like Shepherd. So. A few months ago reports began coming in that he'd found something possibly dangerous. All we had was rumors. Nothing concrete. First thought: just talk, just theory. But we put a special team on Shepherd. They found nothing. Only rumors. But the rumor was this: that a genetic weapon was possible. A genetic *weapon*."

"Yes," Corelli was nodding.

"You heard about that?"

"In long talks, yes, over a drink, yes"—Corelli pursed his mouth—"But I never knew, I never knew."

"Right. Well, neither did we. We didn't take it seriously. But we did make an attempt to move in. And got nowhere. We were working on it when this thing happened."

"This thing. A genetic weapon?"

"Wait a minute. All we knew, all the rumors, all they said was that Shepherd had found something that might be able to kill off different genes—hell, I don't know, different kinds of people. Point was, maybe some black will get hold of it and want to kill off whites, or vice versa, or maybe even the Chinese would develop the thing and kill off everybody, or maybe you'd get only the people with blue eyes, but what the hell, we couldn't take it too seriously, but we did follow the guy. We did our best. You know those guys. Hell, Corelli knows. There's a bunch of scientific types who call themselves 'international,' like that Club of Rome. The guys who want to work outside their country, and have already voted not to give any more dangerous information to their own governments. They don't trust politicians." Hiller grinned, chortled.

Ring said, "The Club of Rome. That's where Shepherd came from."

"Yes."

"That's where the town dies."

"Point two." Hiller raised two fat fingers. "Shepherd had friends there. Close friends. They knew a little about what he was doing. But nobody would talk. So, we were following. The man in Rome, well, we had sent a team in yesterday to pick him up. The team . . . is dead."

A moment of silence. Hiller said, "Point three. We have a team that works only on radio frequencies. You know, short-wave contact. Well, they began to pick up talk coming out of this Zone. Finally ADF-ed it in—to here, to Jefferson. They were getting talk coming out of that dead town. So they sent the word upstairs, but by the time we found out it was late yesterday and the talk was in Italian, and it was scientific, so it took us time to tape it and also to find somebody who knew what the man was saying, and we only had a little of it, but now it's clear it was Shepherd talking, and he was trying to explain to some of his friends what had happened. And he was speaking Italian to somebody in Rome. And that's where the next thing went off. And now Rome is dead."

At that moment Corelli crossed himself. His face had gone pale. Armitage said, "Shepherd's friends. How many people know what he's doing?"

Hiller said, "We're moving in. Fast as we can. He only has a few. We'll get them."

Corelli said, "The thing in Rome . . . is it the same type of radiation? Heavy radiation?"

Hiller said, "Who the hell knows?"

"Is it moving?"

169

"No. Not that I know, thank God. It's stable. Right now. But who the hell knows? Jesus. Three million people. I mean, Jesus, how do you hit *Rome*? How can you blow up St. Pete's church? Christ, look at the Catholics all over the world . . . but how else can you stop that damned thing?"

Armitage said, "We'll hit this one."

Corelli, rubbing his face, said, "I need a drink."

Hiller said, "Me too. Thank God this ain't the Italian government. They're hysterical. What's left of them. But Rome's not our problem. Thank God. Here we can hit, and buddy, we'll hit *here*, if Shepherd doesn't turn the thing off."

"So." Ring stood up. "So. Are you sure of that? At least that? He can turn the thing off."

"Yup. If he wants to. So we'll have to make him want to. Or we hit. Talk to him on the radio. Any way you can. Soon as you can."

Corelli said, "But what if it happens in another town?"

Hiller said, "I need a drink."

Corelli said, "What about Washington?"

Hiller looked at him. Then he said slowly, "One great advantage. The thing's a perfect circle. Armitage calls it . . . 'The Fountain.' The thing in Rome is a solid circle. So there's a source in the center. A small thing in the center. So. We know where to hit. We have ourselves a clear target. So we'll hit. Nuclear, if necessary. But we can stop it. Believe me, friend, we will. It's only a matter of time. And in the morning we'll tell Shepherd to move, and if he doesn't we know *this*—that the source of the damned thing isn't permanent, it's a man-made gadget, a goddamned machine—and by order of the President we'll blow it to hell and gone. What the Italians do is up to them. We'll help if they ask. But this one, by Christ, we'll blow."

Corelli crossed himself. His eyes were wide. Corelli said, "It's a war."

* * *

A cold night. The sky was clearing. Ring stood on a strange porch looking up into the black sky. Armitage touched his shoulder and said, "Go to sleep. Take a break."

"Not now."

"Well, then, let's go check out the RAV. See how they're doing. Hee. It gets interesting. Kind of boring when there's not even a small war."

"See you in a moment. Corelli?"

The small man was walking by, wandering, head down, hands in his pockets. Ring said, "Corelli. Want to talk to you."

Armitage moved off. Corelli said, "I could use a drink. You mind?"

"The dossier on Shepherd. Anything come in?"

"Not yet."

"There's not a hell of a lot of time. Listen. What do you know about the man?"

"Not much."

"But you're always . . . scared. That right? Why? What do you know?"

"I didn't know him. I heard some things about him. I only saw him a few times."

Ring took him by the arm. "Let's go get a drink. Where did you see him?"

"At Berkeley. He taught there for a while. After the Nobel." Corelli shook his head. "You really have to . . . *see* the man. Listen to him talk. He could talk, all right. Sure could. His lectures were . . . very strong. Students got to following him around, like young disciples. They really did. He never asked for it. He was a . . . what you call a 'loner.' He did most of his work alone. No committees. He shied away from groups. They called him 'The Herald.' That was his nickname. 'The Herald of the Lightning.' That's what some student called him. It stuck."

"The Herald."

"Quote from Nietzsche."

"Nietzsche. You mean . . . what do you mean?"

"No, I don't think he was a fanatic. He was . . . a geneticist. He believed like Nietzsche, that man is an imperfect beast, a step in evolution on the way upward. Many men think that way, you know, even the religious ones like Chardin. But Shepherd was . . . *is* a scientist. He thought that the goal of genetics was to get rid of human weakness . . . inherited sickness, stupidity, all human weakness. In that way he thought Nietzsche was right. Modern man is not the end of the line. So they called him 'The Herald.' And began agreeing with him. But he never formed any club, never joined anything. He was an independent man. He was against . . . the collective mind. He said . . . the world was becoming a beehive. He said once, I remember this: 'no way to reason with the collective mind, no way to be free from the group. The only solution, in the end, is that one will destroy the other.' "

Ring walked in the dark, trying to see Corelli's face.

"You're afraid of him. Is that why?"

"Well."

"Go on."

Corelli stopped in the dark. "Because . . . he thought the great weakness in all life was the imperfect man. It was not the government or the system or even the laws. No matter the government, the wars go on. The murders go on. The sickness and stupidity and incompetence go on, and no law will cure them. Education won't. That's what he believed. The problem is *us*. You and me, Richard, you and me." Corelli grunted, threw up his hands. "The problem is . . . what are we really worth? What is the value of man? Not money. God knows. Not power. How many of us . . . are of value to each other? How many make the world any better, any happier? He . . . Shepherd thought the greatest weakness of the created world was the Common Man. And when I listened to him . . . I had to think about it. And in the end, you know, I began to agree."

They came to Ring's dark house. They stopped in the dark. Corelli said, "I think I'll lie down."

"Yes. You better. But . . . one thing. You never answered the question. What do you fear?"

"I see the end coming."

"What? What end?"

"Because *he's* the power. Shepherd's the power. Not the army anymore. Not any government. The weapon is not muscle anymore, not masses, not even armies. The new force that's coming comes out of the brain, as the bomb did, as penicillin, as poison gas . . . right this moment. Over there" —Corelli waved into the dark—"he's sitting. Over there. And he's sorry for me, and doesn't hate me. He doesn't hate anybody. It's not my fault that I'm not very bright, nowhere near as useful as him. I'll never win a Nobel, that's for sure, but it's not my fault. And that's one reason the Soviets hate the Nobel, but . . . I'll never earn much, or govern much, or create much, be of much value to anybody anywhere, and when I die I'll soon be forgotten, like all the other animals, like all the dead trees . . . but none of that is my fault. I was . . . born that way. But . . . the future is not mine. And the future is coming. I'm . . . obsolete, old friend. I'm obsolete."

Ring stared at the dark face for a long moment. Then he said, "Go to sleep."

"I will. I will. But you know the strangest thing? The man in there . . . I think he's right. You and me . . . have so little of value. And you know . . . I don't mind if he wins the war. I don't mind."

"He won't. Go to sleep."

"Oh, yes he will. If he wants to. That's what I'm sure of. That's why I'm afraid."

Corelli wandered off into the dark.

A little man, a chilling night. Ring shuddered. We'll hit, we'll hit. The beauty of the job had always been . . . the power. If we ever wanted to hit, break them, we could always break them.

He could not go to sleep. He sat for a while in the dark, smoking. Why the Soviets hate the Nobel. Never thought of that. You must no longer reward the gifted man. The Herald . . . of the Lightning.

Ring went out into the night with Armitage. Armitage chatted; Ring did not listen. There was the Wall out there and a thing growing behind it and he had known all along there was something new there, something on earth that had not been there before, a personal weapon, a huge weapon, a thing at last in the hands of a single man: the man who could push the button. And the thing Ring had known all along was that he did not understand what was going on back there, and he would begin to understand now that he never would, that the damned thing in there was beyond him, that all of it was coming to the world as a gigantic surprise, the way all the great weapons do, the way the rifle was a booming shock to the dying Indian, the way the mushrooming bomb astounded the pilot of the dropping plane. Ring walked into the coming dawn with a calming, freezing brain. Will be interesting now, and probably fatal, to see what comes. The equality of man. Did not believe in that anymore. Did as a child . . . thou shalt love thy neighbor . . . but not anymore. But . . . what about you, Richard?

Obsolete?

Armitage said, "We can move right now. Anytime you want."

"Yes."

"Well, when do you think we'll move?"

"Ask Hiller."

"Sure, but when do you think? Because, boy, we can blow that thing to hell and gone in no time at all."

"Goddamn." Ring rubbed his eyes. He saw in his mind the face of Nick Tesla. Something of value. What was the value? What was . . . the point? Was there any point at all? Or was it the way they used to teach and teach: the world was created, as Voltaire once said, to drive men mad. "Goddamn," Ring said again. Then he said, "I'm sleepy."

"Well, there they are."

Armitage pointed.

Ring saw: a silvery tank. Long, low silvery tank. Long lean cannon.

Armitage said, "That there is Number One. We'll have a camera in that one and we'll guide it and it'll be armed, of course, and nothing in there can hurt it. We'll mount some shells . . . don't know how many yet, but enough, enough. Well, what do you think? Take a good look."

Ring moved past a watchful soldier, who saluted. He put out a hand, touched cold metal. Silver? Armitage said joyfully, "We've got six more of these babies, but this is the only one ready now. So. What do you think? We have to wait a few hours to send 'em all in."

Ring shook his head. A tank was a thing of power: metal, inhuman. There'd be no brain inside the tank. Nothing of value. Armitage said, "Well, this one of course will lead the way, and the RAV will follow, and the camera inside will see it all. So. You know the plan."

"What the hell do I know?"

Armitage peered. Ring said, "Explain."

"Well"—Armitage pointed—"there's the RAV." The thing sat to the right, in the darkness behind the tank, a white metal truck. It was larger than the tank, taller, a large aluminum box, with wheels. Armitage said, "Now, that there thing will blow like hell. It's loaded. It's a little touchy, but with the tank in front of it, hell, all we have to do is move in, and the tank clears the way. You follow me?" But he went right on chatting, moving toward the RAV, the demolition truck, waving his hands, pointing at imaginary targets.

"Whole point is this: we know where Huston's office was. We know the building. It was the building Nick Tesla was going toward when they shot at him. So we know where the gadget is. And to be exact, we've imported some people, mainly professors, but even one ROTC boss who used to work at that school, and they'll be watching the cameras and can direct us right to the building, and when we get there we'll open up first with the tank and blow a hole through the place, then we'll send the truck in through the hole and blow the whole damned building. And I mean the *whole* building. Because we've got a few tons . . ." He paused, looked at Ring intently. "Any questions?"

Ring leaned against the massive tank. Armitage said, "So we don't really need the kid, the Tesla kid. Not anymore."

Ring said nothing. He thought: warn the kid. Armitage said, "So there it is. Ready to go. Only thing that can stop it, as I understand it, is if Shepherd is reached, and will turn the thing off. Well, there's no word from Shepherd. But he knows, he knows. Still, we'll keep men on the fringe of the Zone and if the radiation stops at any time we'll stop any assault. So. That's the plan. How does it look?"

"Fine." But something burned in Ring's brain: something of heat. Sleepless? But there was a black thing rising in the back of the mind, a big blot, slumbering: vacant memory of an evil dream. And there was another part of the mind, the murderous mind, that wanted to be *in* the tank, to go in and see . . . he saw the machine gun on top of the tank: a tiny turret. He said, pointing, "How about that?"

Armitage looked. Ring said, "Can you fire that?"

Armitage grunted.

Ring said, "Is that under remote control, like the cannon?"

"Um. Didn't think it was . . . necessary."

"It may be."

Armitage hand to his mouth, said, "See what you mean."

"They may try to defend the place."

"I'll be damned!"

"A possibility." Ring was thinking: the new terrorist. Shepherd? But his practical mind moved practically ahead, saw the possibility.

Armitage said, "What the hell could they do?"

"Could have mined the place, knowing you were coming."

Armitage, wide-eyed, said, "You don't really think . . ."

"But the main point is, your lenses. Your antenna. If they hit your lenses, we can't see. The antenna, how do you move?"

"Um. Well, but . . . do I have the authority?"

"Arm the machine gun. I'll go to Hiller. Point is, that building has killed seventy thousand people. Possibility is that Shepherd may defend it. Must think of that. There may be a plan here."

"Hey."

He turned, saw Corelli, wandering in the night. He raised a hand in a formal, whiskey salute. He said formally, happily, "Good evening, gentlemen."

"*Ciao*," said Armitage.

"Thought you gentlemen might be interested in the latest news."

"What?"

"Our friend in Rome?"

"What news?"

"Rome, Italy," Corelli said with one raised finger. "Not Rome, Georgia. Remember that town? Across the pond?"

"What?" Try to be patient. He's drunk.

"Well, I just heard, gentlemen, a pleasant word, and thought you gentlemen would like to know, so I came wandering here toward the powers that be." He paused, waved both hands. "Rome is open."

Armitage said, "Open?"

"Radiation has ceased," Corelli said, nodded, raised his glass sagely. "The thing in there quit working."

Armitage said, "Hey."

"What happened? Do you know what happened?" Ring asked.

Corelli grinned. "The power quit."

"What power?"

Corelli went on smiling. "The Roman power." He hiccuped. "He. You've got to know good old Rome. I was born near there. Power in that town, hic, is a newfangled gadget. It always quits. Hee."

"But, the thing doesn't go on working, that what you mean?"

"Right. Check. Salute!" Corelli drank.

"Damn." Armitage was cheered.

Ring said, "The man who turned it on. Do they know who it was?"

"Oh, him. He's dead," Corelli said.

"Dead. You're sure? How come?"

"He died because he turned the thing on. After it killed him, it went on running for a while, and then ran out of power. Hic. Thass how it worketh."

"So. It's done. That's how it ends." Ring turned toward the Wall. He said, "Shepherd was talking to a man in Rome. Who else? Where else?"

Armitage said, "We'll be in there soon. A matter of time."

Ring looked east, saw the first break in the dark, the far small glow of the coming dawn. Corelli said dreamily, "If only *I* . . . could live in there. . . ."

EIGHT

He dreamed of women: he woke to a kiss.

Her hair touched his face. She was laughing. He came slowly up out of the dark and saw a sun-blazed window and her hair above his eyes and beyond that the wood-beamed ceiling. She kissed him on the nose, giggled. He felt himself begin to smile. A moment later he had coffee in his hand. He began to focus: a beautiful smiling girl. Sunlight in a cabin. O brave new world. Dirty dreams. She said, "My, but you sleep late. Do you do that all the time?"

"Um?"

"I was up early. I just couldn't sleep. I was up at dawn and I went out there and drove around and it was absolutely delightful. I met people. I had coffee with a couple, and I met this really pretty girl, a little older than I am, and that priest again, that Jesuit, and we had a charming breakfast. And I came back but you were still asleep. When did you go to sleep?"

"Not until almost dawn."

"Are you a night owl?"

"Um."

"Oh. Dr. Shepherd was just here. A little while ago. He wants to talk to you. He said he'll be back."

"Shepherd."

"Dr. Shepherd." She was looking at Nick's face with adoring eyes. Nick said, "He knows they want to talk to him."

Ruth nodded.

"What did he say?"

"He said he doesn't want to talk to them."

"Um. You told him it was a Presidential order."

Ruth smiled. "He didn't seem to care about that. He . . . wants to talk to you. He says it's important. He says he'll be back soon." She folded her arms, smiled a curious smile. "Impressive man."

"You were impressed?" Nick was suddenly jealous, knew it, felt like a fool, swallowed it. Nobel?

"He won't talk to the President," Ruth said. "And he doesn't have to. And when you think about that, it's impressive. Oh, when I talked to that Jesuit again, we went in to the story of Noah again, of God cursing the masses, you remember, and the Jesuit was *fascinating*, really, he kept trying to figure out what really happened, if there really was a Noah, and if this thing that happened here was a judgment of God. I thought he was a little, well, flaky, but, when you think about it, and you heard about Rome, you begin to wonder . . . if there's a point. Well, now, do you want some breakfast? More coffee? Saint Nick?"

She popped forward, kissed him again on the cheek. She was a very happy girl. It was a charming day. Nick said, "Don't do that again. I'm in the bed, and I may grab. There are no cops anymore. Prepare to defend yourself."

He was kidding, but she looked at him, backed away. Then she smiled, put one hand in her hair, fluffed it, turned, giggled, hopped outside.

They had breakfast ondeck. It was long after dawn, almost ten o'clock. He knew he should talk to Ring, but he didn't for a while. He sat there having eggs on a lovely day in a silent sunlit town and while they were talking about making some plans for the day, maybe to go out to the airport and fly, he heard a noise: sound of an engine a long way away, and looked, and there in the distance around a bend came a car, a convertible: yellow, the top down. The car came down the street toward the marina, and Nick could see the head of a blonde woman, hair flowing outward in the light wind, and she turned near the marina, slowed, waved, and then went out of sight. Ruth said, "That's the one I saw this morning." She was watching Nick carefully. "She's rather cute."

"Didn't really see."

Ruth said, smiling, "We are not alone."

"Sure aren't."

A few moments later, another car, dark blue, at the top of the hill. It passed out of sight. Nick said, "Gee. The town's getting crowded."

"Just enough."

"You're not . . . lonely."

She looked at him. "Not at all." After a moment she said, dismayed, "Are you?"

"Well, I guess not."

She watched him, smiled, again moved a hand beautifully, delicately, through her dark brown red-streaked hair. "Have to make it more cozy, Saint Nick."

Nick said, "Don't kid."

She smiled, winked.

Nick said, "Well, I guess I've got to call Ring."

"Do you have to? I mean"—she was suddenly charmingly haughty—"if Shepherd won't talk to the *President* . . ."

"We could take the boat out for a while."

Ruth said, "You're a free man."

Nick said wistfully, "I really ought to call him."

Ruth sighed. "Saint Nick."

"That's me."

"An honest man."

"That's me. Sexy as hell, but honest."

He picked up the radio. Ring came on almost instantly, was obviously annoyed. Nick sensed that other world out there—that massive, busy, noisy, crowded world, unreal until now—until the sound of Ring's voice. Strange, strange sensation: reality in a thin voice.

Ring said, "Have you seen that Shepherd?"

"Nope. Well, he was here earlier, but I was asleep."

"He was *there*?"

"Yep."

"Does he know we want to talk to him?"

"Yep. I think he does."

"Well, dammit, what's going on?"

"He said he'll be back here in a little while."

"Well, now, listen. We've got to talk to him. Because things are about to happen. Stay right on this tube, sonny, because it could get rather sticky."

"Sticky?"

"We've got to talk to Shepherd. That thing in that town is going to be turned off. He's got to know that."

"Well, I'll tell him. Soon as I can."

"Tell him to talk to us. Keep that radio open. This is by direct order of the President. If you want to, you can speak to him. He'll be on it in a few minutes, whenever necessary. But it's a Presidential order. That you understand."

"Yep."

"Because listen, kid, things could get dangerous in that place. If we have to blow it . . . well. Things are about to happen."

A car came around the bend.

A white police car.

Nick said, "Wait a minute. I think he's coming."

"Well, keep this open, keep it open. He's got to talk."

Ring went on; Nick lowered the volume. The police car came to the marina gate, stopped, three men got out. The first crowd Nick had yet seen. The tall man was Shepherd. One of the others was tall and thin and white-haired, older;

184

the second was short and chubby and much younger, younger perhaps than Nick. All three men were armed around the waist. They all waved a formal hello. Shepherd came slowly through the gate and down the walk. He was wearing the same gray sweater, but now he had a belted holster around his hips; a big gun hung there as in the days of the old West. There was something indescribably impressive about the man. He came on slowly, the gray gun bobbing at his hip, like an old old hero from an ancient movie. The voice of Ring was rattling on in the background about what was happening. Nick told him to hold on a moment, turned the voice down.

Shepherd came up to the rail. He raised one hand, smiled a tired smile.

"Morning, skipper. Can I come aboard?"

"Sure." Nick opened the rail. The two men up there got back into their car. Shepherd said, with a vague trace of apology, "Those fellas are listening to the radio. Have to keep in touch. But . . . want to talk to you. Few minutes. Do you mind? Rather important."

"Go ahead and sit down. But"—Nick held out the black hand radio—"you must know they want to talk to you."

"Not now." Shepherd sat on a deck chair.

"Listen. Do you know what you're up against?"

Shepherd nodded. "Not now," he said. He pointed at the radio in Nick's hand. "I want to talk to you alone for a few minutes. After that . . . do what you will. But . . . could you turn that thing off? For a little while?"

Nick stood there for a moment, looked at the radio. He turned it off. The thing began beeping. He tucked it in the toolbox on deck, closed the lid, cut off the sound.

Shepherd said, "I appreciate that." He leaned forward, elbows on his knees, a tired man.

Ruth said, "Can I get you anything?"

"Very kind," Shepherd said.

"Coffee? Brandy?" Ruth gave that lovely smile. "I'm temporary hostess of the temporary ship."

Nick said, "Listen. Just want to make sure you know. They can hit here anytime. They're zeroed in. Hope that's clear."

Shepherd looked up at Nick. "Is that clear to you?"

"Me?"

"Then why do you stay?"

"Well."

"Do you like it here? How long would you like it here?"

Nick said nothing, watching. The man's face was . . . intense. Shepherd looked out over the river. He said slowly, "Seventy thousand dead. Can't give it back to them. Not now. It makes no difference now. I didn't kill them. Understand. I didn't do that. But it's done. Seven days. Must sit here and think. Must never judge too soon, too soon."

Nick sat waiting. Something coming. Shepherd looked back. His voice was slow and clear: he was sending his message. "Might's well get to the point. There's a machine in this town that killed all those people. The machine is still working. As long as it continues sending out its own selective radiation, nobody can come into this town except a few, a very few. Chosen few. Whether that's an accident or not I don't yet know. We live by accident and die by accident, or we live by plan and die by plan. You and I are alive and seventy thousand are dead. If there's any plan at all beyond life, we're here for a reason. If there isn't . . ."

Shepherd paused. He was speaking with great, quiet intensity, like a dedicated priest. Nick felt a crawling chill. He listened. Shepherd said, "I'm not going to open the gate."

He looked back and forth from face to face.

"Many reasons, I hope . . . you'll understand. Main thing is: I can't help the dead. But I can keep this place free. I have a weapon here that they'll all want outside, and some already have, and one man in Rome has already used, and I can't give the thing away. If I open the gate and the government comes in . . . we'll no longer be free. Neither you nor I. The government will be there to control your life, no longer leaving it up to you, to me, but more than that: the governments all over the world are moving in on research. They'll stick their guns into the research, into all the research, and in doing that they'll end all progress, they'll end the growth of knowledge, all out of fear of it, they'll end any hope of a better world. But . . . we can have a free place here for a while at least, and so . . . that's the way it will stay. I've thought for seven days. It's my choice. I've made it."

Nick went on sitting for a long moment, motionless, then whistled. He looked up toward the police car and saw the two men were standing out in the open, holding rifles. Was it them who shot? Nick said slowly, "You can't . . . hold on to this place . . . against the Army."

"Yes, I can." Shepherd sat without moving, gazing at Nick. He nodded. "That's the heart of the matter. That's the point. They have a weapon. I have a weapon. Hope they understand that. Don't know if they can. That's why I wanted to talk to you, explain it to you. Son, things here are rather dangerous. I know that. I know they can hit me. But if they do, I can hit back. And I will. I won't tell them how, but I want them to know that. I want them to leave me alone. I want this place to be left free. I don't know how long. I don't even know how long we'll go on living here. But I do know this and I want the Army outside to know it, and I'm not going to explain it: if there's any threat to me, I will reply. *I will reply.*"

After a moment Ruth stood up, wrapped her arms around her waist. "Wow!" she said.

Shepherd watched.

Nick said, "Look. What's happening?"

Shepherd shook his head.

"What do you mean, you will reply?"

187

"I won't explain. Not now. Hope you understand. Don't want to give them any advantage. I have . . . another weapon."

Nick said, "Jesus!"

"You can leave anytime, son. If you want to stay . . . that's up to you. Just wanted you to know . . . the facts. Now, excuse me a moment."

Shepherd moved off the boat, headed up toward the two men at the police car. Nick stood alone with Ruth. Ruth stood hunched, her arms around her chest, staring at Nick. She said, "What do you think?"

Nick shook his head. Ruth said, "Just to be left alone. He isn't asking much."

"I guess . . . maybe . . ."

Ruth said, very softly, "A new world. What would we need here? You and I? If we live here together, you and I? We could take care of each other. All we need is each other."

Nick took a deep breath.

Ruth said, "I would try to help you. If you needed me."

Nick said, "Well."

"Would you need me?"

"Yep."

"Really?"

"Yep."

"He says . . . it wouldn't last long. But just for a while . . . some time here, alone. Quiet world. No more crowds. No more . . . society. No more rules. Free. He said that. *Free.* The way I . . . never was."

Shepherd was coming back. Nick looked up. He had a paralyzed moment; could not think, could not feel, could not speak. But he saw strain on Shepherd's face. Tension. He said, "What's up?"

Shepherd stopped at the railing, put both hands down, stared, pursed his lips.

Nick said, "If you could explain some of it. I'd like to know . . . *something.*"

Shepherd looked up with tired eyes. "Not much time." He shook his head, fluttered the gray hair. "Let it be. Let it be."

"What's happening? Did something go wrong?"

"I was always so proud," Shepherd said. He gazed out across the river. "Too proud, as they say. Well, time to get on."

He was gripping the railing, both hands whitening at the knuckles. He said slowly, "My goal was . . . to make a better man. That sounds awful . . . to many people. Are you happy with Man the way he is? Ah, no matter. But when I was a young man I saw work I could do that could be . . . something fine. I saw that we were steadily conquering the bad food, the dangerous germ, we'd slain hunger, the virus was under attack. So I went out against the gene: the murdering gene. And you know, *even now,* I still think it must be done. And it will."

He paused, glanced back at Nick. "Look around you. There's one answer." He put his hand to his eyes, rubbed. His voice was soft but of extraordinary intensity.

"May not see you again, son. Best I can do . . . tell you what happened. You be the judge." He turned, looked out to sea. "I came across this . . . thing . . . some years ago. I was studying human tissue, cells of people with major genetic defects. I was trying to understand how to . . . cure that. I have no major genetic defect myself. I knew long ago, after . . . an accident . . . that I had a strong resistance to radiation. I didn't know why. Nobody could tell me. Point begins . . . with that. An unfair world. So much of his trouble is born into Man. I could never accept that. An unfair God, who gave some men great health and sight and kidneys and fine hearts, and others . . . no kidneys at all, no sight at all, no arms at all, ears that would never hear, brains that could never think. . . . Well, I had a goal. I was trying to find a way to straighten genetic defects: to iron out the wrinkle. I was trying to . . . fix it." He breathed slowly, hunched. "I found . . . just the opposite." He held on to the railing, gripping for a long moment, glanced once at Nick, shrugged. "I don't want to explain this technically. For your sake. But . . . I can tell you a few things. I found . . . a substance. A molecular structure. That suddenly had something I never expected, I never saw coming, it had suddenly . . . great power. In a way I . . . can't explain. But what it did was blow out a burst that seemed to affect the tissue of a genetically defective body. That's . . . all I can say. It seemed to have no effect on tissue that was, I knew, from a source with no known defect. It seemed to be a *cure*. But . . . of what? I didn't know. So I went to work. Most of it I did alone, but some students . . . and the damned thing blossomed. No, no. It went off like a blooming *bomb*. It killed a . . . defective cell. Then I saw that it destroyed not only that one cell but others around me. In a way I didn't understand. It seemed to murder some tissue instantly, shrivel it, but others . . . it left alone. As if they were negative and the power was negative, and it couldn't touch . . . and I went on working, and didn't know what I was developing, and the damned thing . . . could be made very, very strong. Very strong. It went through walls. It went out . . . I thought at first it destroyed only defective tissue, genetically defective. But, I knew, almost everyone has something . . . so I stopped. I told many friends. But I stopped. And they didn't." Shepherd nodded. "You see? You see? There are many people . . . out there . . . who went on working. I didn't understand. The thing was too dangerous to test. I stopped. Tried to think. Think it through. And then Dave Huston left the Coast and came out here to work and started his own research in his own Lab. And you know?" Shepherd gave a soft, wry smile. "I got him the job. I recommended him. Fine boy. Fine. Worked all the time, always until late at night . . . trying to build a better man. Well, you never knew Dave. He had no . . . respect for man. He was . . . moody. He was certain the world was heading toward disaster: nuclear war, overpopulation, political intrusion. The new Dark Age. He thought the only goal was to change the coming disaster by changing man. He was fired with hope, and so he came here to research genetics, and he began to experiment with the . . . substance. He began building a machine. He didn't talk about it. He wanted to cure things like retardation, cystic fibrosis, the psychopathic mind, but he didn't talk about it. Men don't like the idea of scientists tinkering with their God-given genes. With the arm, perhaps, the heart, yes, but not the brain. They want to be . . . left alone . . ."

Shepherd stopped. He was suddenly restless. He stood, rubbed his hands together. His face was sharper.

"Well, get to the point old man. Dave Huston built the thing here: a device putting out radioactive beams, aimed at defective genetic structure. He began getting results with very small tests. He hadn't yet turned the thing on. He called it 'The Big D.' He wired me, in Rome. I came as quickly as I could. He'd already killed some people, and knew it, but no one else did. No one in this town. Although the government was closing in and he knew that too. He wanted to talk to me once, just once, so we sat down late at night and talked until midnight, but I was on Rome time and tired, because to me . . . to me it was dawn . . . but I remember, I remember . . . Huston knew the thing didn't cure; the thing killed. But that last night . . . he had begun to believe it was mercy killing. He'd removed a sickness. He began to believe that he'd been given the only possible answer to a nightmare future. He thought he could make a better world, a healthy world. He knew he'd kill himself." Shepherd nodded: dreaming eyes. "He knew that. He knew he'd leave some of

191

us, only a few, how many he never knew, I never knew. But the few left he thought would be . . . survival of the fittest? God's will? Ah." Shepherd slowly slowly shook his head. "Oh, yes, he had it reasoned out. O brave new world, that has such people . . . I listened. I didn't argue. Because the more I learned, you see"—he turned his weary eyes, blinked—"the more I knew that I didn't know. Will . . . never know. Ah. Well, I didn't argue. I didn't think he was insane. I don't think so now. I just sat there late that night and we talked, for the last time, although I didn't know that, and I remember asking him about himself, you, Dave, you, and I remember him smiling and shrugging and saying, *oh, hell, I'll never last. I don't know about you, old buddy, maybe there's hope for you, but me? Hell, man. I have many defects. The eyes alone . . . .*"

Shepherd raised his hands. "So he knew he was killing himself. Before he ever pushed the button. He never knew how many he would kill. He knew . . . the government was closing in on him. He knew that. I asked him . . . to think about it. That's all I said. I didn't expect . . . anything. I went to bed. At 2 A.M. he went back to the Lab and wrote me a note and turned the thing on. Maximum thrust." A moment of silence. Shepherd stared at nothing. "And so he died in the Lab. He wrote me a note . . . I don't know why he expected me to live. Why me. Neither of us ever expected . . . so many to die. In the note he wrote, 'Either we live by plan and die by plan, or live by accident and die by accident.' That was . . . Thornton Wilder, I think. And so. I woke up. I woke up. To my own . . . everlasting . . . surprise." A long silence. The face of a weary man, but gentler now, almost at rest.

Nick sat watching him. He was . . . in awe of the man. Slowly he said, "Well, one thing I'm glad of . . . I'm sure glad it wasn't *you*, not you . . . who turned the damned thing on."

"Doesn't matter." Voice of Ruth. Nick turned. She was sitting upright, stiff-backed, hands clenched together, gazing at Shepherd. She said, "It really doesn't matter. I understand. I think."

Shepherd turned the dark eyes toward her: stared, slowly nodded. Then he said, "Point is . . . I couldn't turn it off. The Big D. You . . . know that? Yes. That morning I went into the Lab . . . and I knew. Only thing I didn't know was . . . how many were dead. So many." He blinked. "Didn't expect that many. Didn't expect . . . myself." He opened his eyes wide. "I just sat there . . . trying to understand. I sat . . . all that day. Right by his body. Dave and I. I sat all day and at the end . . . I couldn't turn the thing off."

He put his hands together, in the form of a prayer, held them against his chin. "I thought . . . God's will be done. I may have gone a little . . . outside. Thinking of what was coming. I saw all this coming, you see. The armies. The fingers on the buttons . . ."

He stopped, rubbed his eyes. Then he shook his head quickly, trying to clear the brain. He looked back suddenly with a rare irony in his eyes.

"I was expecting some news from my friends. Oh, yes. The man in Rome. He knew he would die, just as Dave Huston did. But he thought it was time to take a stand. Like Huston . . . clean up the world. There are men like that . . . all over the world, who hate nations and races and if there was a button to push . . . so I sat there . . . and couldn't open the gate. No. You know I . . . thought for years that some fanatic would get enough uranium together someday, sooner or later, and blow up . . . London? But what's out there is no fanatic. What's out there is . . . Man. The world out there may be sick. It's certainly bloody. And almost never . . . free."

Nick sat in a moment of thundering silence. He remembered that night in the desert looking up at the fragmented sky, the white stars, waiting for the message, the voice that never came. After a while he said, "All right. Want to make it clear. Why me? You and me? Why?"

"Adaptation."

"What? You mean . . . hell, what do you mean?"

Shepherd answered slowly. His voice was colder now; his mind was backing away. He said, "The human body adapts. It learns, and changes. Just how it does that, and why so many fail"—he shrugged—"but when something dangerous appears, and threatens, the human body fights back, or learns to adapt, in order to survive. One day something happened. But . . . radiation has always been out there. So when it happened . . . it may be that there are only a very few people like us on all Earth, in a few places, near exposure to massive radiation which has been there only in the last century. But it may also be that a small band of Bushmen living over the rich uranium down in South Africa adapted to it long ago, thousands of years ago, and will survive this thing today, when everyone near them dies. It may be that radium, or cosmic radiation . . . no way yet to tell. Why us? You and I. Ah. We are . . . a genetic fluke. Or perhaps Darwin was right and we fit the pattern: survival of the . . . fittest. Accident? Or plan. I think of that myself . . . almost all the time. I think all night long. Hail Mary, full of grace. God . . . is with thee."

Nick chilled, looked at Ruth, her face gone blank. He thought: God be with thee. He looked up at the white sky.

Shepherd was looking past Nick up the hill. Ruth said something Nick didn't hear. He focused on the toolbox. Radio in there. Ah. Ring won't like this.

Well, who will?

Ruth.

He looked at the radiant girl. Well constructed. No flaw.

She needs me.

Nick felt a shudder.

Shepherd was saying, ". . . talked for a long time. Told them all I told you. They made a choice. They want to be left alone."

He had pointed to the two men up the road. Nick turned to look that way. Shepherd said, "The older man there reads philosophy. Do you know him? I thought not. He was talking last night about Pascal's Wager. Do you remember that?"

Nick heard a new sound in the far distance.

Shepherd said, "Pascal's Wager is this: if a man believes in God, any God, follows all the rules until he dies, and then turns out to be wrong . . . what a shame. But . . . if a man doesn't believe in God, any God, and therefore lives all his life with no rules at all to follow, no good, no evil, until he dies . . . what if *he* turns out to be wrong, ah, what then?"

The noise was louder: something coming. Large engine. Shepherd seemed not to hear. The two men up the road had come out of the car, yelled, waved, pointed.

Roar of an engine. Nick knew. Big metal. Diesel.

The long tank swung into view at the top of the hill.

Long silver tank with a long sleek cannon.

Shepherd ran back to his car.

The thing turned left, was moving toward the school. There was another thing behind it: a white truck. Nick saw: Shepherd's car moving, heading up the road, off to the left. Gone in a moment, and the tank and the truck gone. Nick said, "Come on." He ran down toward his car. He stopped, waited for Ruth. He thought: don't take her. He said, "You better stay here."

She said no, got in the car on the other side. He turned on the radio, started driving toward the school. He said, "Where the hell is Ring?"

A moment: "Ring here. What's happening?"

"I've just seen a tank. What are you doing?"

"The tank is heading toward the school. We're going to give Shepherd ten minutes to turn that thing in there off. If he doesn't, we'll blow that building. Where's Shepherd?"

"He's gone off in a car. Listen . . ."

"Get him to talk. We'll hold everything if he'll talk."

"Jesus. I'll try."

Nick drove. He came out from under the long row of trees and saw the tank already moving out across the open green where the rifle bullet had just missed him, but he could not see the truck behind it. To the left he saw motion, swerved. Shepherd's car, the men coming out. He looked back at the tank—in motion—the silver gun turret turning toward Shepherd.

* * *

Three television monitors, to the left and center the tank: the right the picture coming in from the RAV. They were clear. The left was turning, wide angle. The professor said, "The third floor, right there. That will be Huston's office. Right there." He went forward, put his finger on the picture.

Ring said, "Wide angle."

The lens shifted. White building. Concrete. The professor, a fat, bearded man, said, "That is undoubtedly correct."

Ring said, "Swivel left."

Slowly left: grass, trees. They saw the car there under a thick tree, men in motion behind a high bush, azaleas. The men were gone.

Hiller said, "Shepherd. Was that Shepherd?"

Corelli said, "Couldn't see."

"Give me the loudspeaker."

Armitage said, "Center on that building. Prepare to fire."

Hiller took the mike in his hand. To Armitage he said, "This thing work?"

"He'll hear you."

"But who the hell was that in the car?"

Ring said, "Tesla's coming. It must have been Shepherd there."

"We can't run after the goddamn car."

Armitage said, "No. Just sit tight. Focus on the building: wide angle left, telescopic right, on the top floors, swing the telescopic, keep turning, but keep the wide angle set. And bring up the RAV to the right, in the rear. We're ready to blow away, anytime."

Hiller said, "Well, turn up the volume."

He held the mike to his mouth, looked at a white concrete building.

* * *

Nick came up behind Shepherd's car, stopped under the willow tree. He saw the two men running away behind the long azalea rows toward the rear of the building. Shepherd stood there by an azalea bush with one hand on his chest, holding himself with the other hand against the tree trunk, staring at the tank. Nick got out of the car. He heard loud and sudden words, huge, metallic, coming out of the tank.

"Dr. Shepherd. Dr. Shepherd. Dr. Shepherd. This is a warning. This is a warning."

The voice was slow and clear: inhuman. Not real. Nick looked at the silver tank, saw the turret rotate slowly left, then right. There was a speaker on the tank. The speaker gave the robot sound: "Dr. Shepherd. Dr. Shepherd. This is a warning. This is a warning. You have five minutes. You have five minutes. You will halt the function of that machine. You will halt the function of that machine. By order of the President of the United States. By order of the President of the United States. You have five minutes. Come out into the open. Come out into the open. You have five minutes. Counting. You have five minutes."

The sound stopped. In the vacant air Nick looked at Shepherd. He stood motionless behind the azalea, watching the tank. He began to lean against the tree. Nick heard the car radio. Ring was saying, "Where's Shepherd?" He could not move. He stood there. He saw one of the men, Shepherd's friend, the tall thin one, come out from the bushes lining the front walk of the building and come crouching around to the front of the tank. The man was carrying a rifle with a scope: black barrel. Nick saw the turret swivel, turning

197

toward the man. The smaller turret of a machine gun turned. The man came forward crouching, toward the front of the tank. Nick heard Ring say something he could not make out, yelling, on the radio. The man crouched and held up the gun and fired at the front of the tank. Nick knew: trying to knock out the camera. A small hole up front. Glass? Must be open. The man fired again. Then moved closer: twenty yards. Nick saw the machine gun turret swivel slightly, flicker: it blasted. A rain of bullets tore through the thin man: he went over leftward and backward, twisting, pieces of the coat flipping out and whirling, red blossoming on his torn face. He was down. On the far side Nick saw motion: the white truck coming out from the trees, saw at the same moment the other Shepherd man, the small young one, standing there with the rifle lifted, waiting; he'd gone around the back of the building and come out the other side, but he was turning now to the new truck, the aluminum truck, and he began firing, one shot after another into the thin window, and Nick saw the machine-gun turret on the tank begin to turn that way, and Nick started to scream, and at that moment the truck blew, disintegrated, blossomed into a red-white cloud, flying metal and glass and grass and dirt, and the blow of hard air pushed Nick like a wave, down, down, rolling, fragments flying by, the sound of collision, and he was thinking of the girl and trying to look up, come into focus, through all the smoke and twisting branches and still flying leaves, and he saw the car still there still sound but the girl nowhere, so he got up and looked in, and she was sitting there with her head down, holding it, and he got in and found she was all right, then he looked through the front window, grazed but not broken, and saw Shepherd down behind the bushes, blood on his face, sitting in the dark under the bush shaking his head.

From the radio came the voice of Ring: "Tesla. Speak to me. What's happening? Tesla!"

Nick held Ruth. She was dazed: untouched. He found blood on his own face. Not deep. Not bad. Torn clothing. No matter. Shepherd? He said to Ruth, "Stay down. Listen, drive the hell out of here. Get out. I've got to look after the man."

He left the car. It didn't move. Ruth sat there. Nick said, "Baby, move!"

He ran toward Shepherd. He saw at that moment: the tank.

It had been thrown against the white building, which was scraped and scarred and flickered with pasted leaves, but undamaged. But the tank was beginning to turn. Nick knelt by Shepherd. Saw blood streaks on his face, a bloody shirt. But no beat, no artery: did not look bad. A bad heart? Shepherd sat with his hand on his chest. Nick said, "Let me get you out of here."

Shepherd nodded. He closed his eyes, opened his eyes, shook his head. He said, "My boys. Ah, why did they do that?"

Shepherd's face was bleeding from the right cheek; he patted it with his hand, looked at the blood. Nick heard the sound of the engine of the tank: turning. Couldn't see it through the bush. He said, taking Shepherd's arm, "Got to get out of here."

"Doesn't really matter." Shepherd looked at blood.

"Come on. I'll help you. You're a big man."

Shepherd shook his head. He started to rise. He took Nick's hand. "I want to get out of here."

Nick helped him. Shepherd said softly, very softly, "They can't blow anything now. Not now. They sent in a detonator, but it had a thin skin." He shook his head, holding his chest. "I knew. I knew. Only a matter of time."

Nick said, "Let me help you."

"Out of sight," Shepherd said. "Out of sight."

Nick let him go. "What do you mean?" he asked.

"Of the tank." Shepherd pointed, over Nick's shoulder.

199

The tank had righted itself. It was turning. It was coming this way. The explosion had only pushed it. The gun was pointed this way. The loudspeaker: "Dr. Shepherd. Dr. Shepherd. You are in our vision. We can see you clearly. Don't move. Don't move. Dr. Shepherd. Don't move."

Shepherd smiled. He reached out a hand, touched Nick's shoulder. Shepherd said, "Good boy. I'll see you."

Shepherd started to walk. He was heading toward his car. Nick saw the tank gun barrel follow him. He screamed, "Don't move!"

Shepherd raised a hand, never turned. He said in a distant voice, "I'm through with all that."

He walked to the car. The loudspeaker: "Dr. Shepherd. Do not move. Do not try to leave. This is your final warning."

Shepherd turned, waved. He got into the car. There was one long second, one long glassy moment with Shepherd sitting there starting the engine and the tank coming and Nick staring motionless, and then the car began to move, slowly, very slowly, only a few feet forward, and the machine gun opened up and the car was hit, the windows blown out, and the car turned and hit a tree.

Nick ran forward. The door was already open. Blood all over one of Shepherd's arms, the right side of his face. He had one hand on the wheel, was looking forward at nothing.

The tank was coming. Blood all over the arm, the chest, pulsing. *He's dying.* The loudspeaker thundered: "Mr. Tesla, we have you in sight. We have you in sight."

The tank was there, a few yards away, bruised and dented: alive.

Nick knelt. The loudspeaker: "Is he dead? Is Dr. Shepherd dead?"

Nick rose, walked toward the tank. The loudspeaker said something. He climbed up onto the track. There was a small square black window, recessing, a small hole, dented. He saw a glass gleam inside. He pointed the .357, fired six times, killed the eye.

* * *

Both monitors were white.

Nothing to see.

Unbelieving, Armitage said, "The *boy* did that!"

Hiller was swearing. Ring thought, mechanically: the RAV was vulnerable. Should have known. He said, "Have to send in something else."

Armitage swore. After a moment Hiller said, "You've got six tanks?"

Armitage nodded.

"How long will it take?"

"Two, three more hours."

"Send them in."

Armitage looked at an officer, the officer was moving.

Hiller said, "That goddamn RAV."

"I just didn't think . . . goddammit," Armitage said.

Hiller said, "So the thing is still on. And you've got a tank sitting there and you can't use it. Jesus." He was thinking of Washington.

Armitage said, "I just never knew there was that kind of resistance."

"What about Shepherd?" Hiller asked.

"He could be dead," Ring said.

Hiller said, "So. How now, goddammit, do you turn the thing off?"

"Nick Tesla," Ring said.

"But it was Tesla . . . who blew the camera."

"Well, but he can't stop the tanks. When they come in, they just start firing. They'll blow through the Wall, and pick the spot, and sooner or later it's got to work. Six tanks together. He can't fight that."

Armitage said, "And the seventh still works. It just can't

see. But it's loaded. Once we get near it, we can aim it from another tank. So." He gleamed. "We'll move in. Fast as possible." He rose, went for the door.

Hiller stared at the vacant monitor. He said, "Try to talk to that kid."

Ring nodded.

"Because, goddammit, you know he's in trouble."

Ring said, "The enemy. Nick's face."

"But if Shepherd's dead . . ."

"Take at least two hours. Then two more to get in there. Will be almost 5 P.M."

"That goddamn RAV. We should have known. Try to get that kid on your radio." Ring tried. Nothing. While he tried he saw an aide give Hiller a message. Hiller put on the glasses, read, crumpled the thing, swore, banged the wall of a radio. Hiller said, "I've got to get out of here."

"You're leaving?"

"Back to Washington."

"What's up?" He sensed something big. He had sensed it all that morning. Hiller shook his head. Then he said, "Got to get out. I'll call. But move. And listen, find out, any way possible, if Shepherd is dead. Because if he is, goddammit, we've been warned. Somebody will hit. Somebody unknown. A friend. We've got to find him. A friend will hit somewhere else. But if Shepherd is dead, do *not* release that information. No. Under no circumstances. Not even to me. Hold till you hear from me. We're finding Shepherd's friends, one by one. But *some* of them, goddammit . . . listen, I've got to go. I'll call."

He was at the door, turned, pointed at Ring with rage. "You *hit* that bastard. Hit with everything you've got. And if that doesn't do it, by Christ, we'll go nuclear. Understand?"

Ring nodded.

Hiller left.

Ring remembered the face of Nick Tesla, young Nick:

hatred, raising a pointed pistol, the last blast. He thought: he's joined the other side.

*　　*　　*

Shepherd was alive. He had taken a bullet through the throat and the right arm and one in the back into a lung. He had cuts of blown glass on his face. They pulled him out onto the grass by the immobile tank and worked, and once Ruth left and turned off the radio, so it was quiet. The right arm was bleeding Shepherd—to death—pumping. Nick took off his belt and put it around Shepherd's arm and helped stem the loss of blood. Shepherd's eyes were open: he was coming back. He said sweetly, like a child, "Thank you very much." Ruth was wiping blood. She ran off, came back with a bucket of water and soap and towels and Nick kept talking about medicine in the drugstore up at the corner, but Shepherd was waking slowly, smiling, his mind at peace, and Nick knew looking at the peace in his eyes that the man was dying and knew it and did not care and Nick went on fighting. Morphine, Demerol, let the man die at least free of pain. But maybe somehow the man could survive. Always that chance. They worked in the afternoon sun. It was a clear day and the air was clean but there was a small fire to the right and one tree was burning and another had been torn down and the roots groped at the sky. Ruth went off to find morphine and something antibiotic. Nick tried talking to Shepherd. He said, "Got to move you, sir."

Shepherd said, "Let me sit up."

Nick helped, got the warm blood on his hands. Shepherd said, "Better get the head up. Ah. Please. Put me against the tree."

Nick did that: a heavy man, but he was resting head high and Nick began to cover the flowing blood asking for instructions now in what to do, because Shepherd sure as hell knew more than he did.

Shepherd said, "Nev' mind. Nev' mind." He lay there

blinking, reached out a wandering left hand. Long, long fingers. "Easy, boy. Easy. All right. Right. Got to rest. Appreciate. Sweet girl." He smiled the boyish smile. His eyes were dimming. But the left hand with the long fingers found Nick's forearm and grasped with strength.

"One thing. Got to tell you. Before. God's will." He looked up, searching for Nick's face, found it, focused, held on, nodded. "Poor kid," he said softly, with great tenderness. "God help you."

"Listen. What can I do?"

"Your choice now. God help you." Shepherd closed his eyes. "If there is a God."

"Look, let me do something. How can I stop the bleeding? Is it an artery? Where?"

Shepherd's eyes opened suddenly, like a light coming on, as if there'd just been a great sound. His grip on Nick's forearm tightened again. He focused on Nick's face. "No time. Got to tell you. Up to you. Now. The thing is up there." He pointed past Nick's shoulder with the other arm. "Up there. Do you know the building? That one? They call it . . . Dietrich. Do you know that?"

Nick looked. Remembered—up there across the way —the Dietrich Lab. "Yes."

Shepherd's face was turning gray. But the light glowed in his eyes. "You know that place, that place up there."

"The Dietrich Lab. Yes. Why?"

"That's where it is."

"You mean . . . the gadget the tank was after? You mean the thing your friend started?"

Shepherd shook his head, gazed at him, took deep breaths, holding him. Nick said, "Easy."

But Shepherd was pushing hard, trying to sit higher. "No time," he said, "no time. No. The thing Huston built . . . is in Huston's Lab. They know that. They'll blow it. But that's not . . ." He was running out of breath, out of strength. He closed his eyes. He seemed to swear, but Nick could not hear the words. He lay for a long moment and Nick saw fresh blood pulsing in his shirt front, coming down out of his throat, and Nick knew in that moment that it was hopeless and then Shepherd said, "In the Lab there, up there . . . the thing I built. I wanted . . . free ground. Somewhere. Permanent. You see? . . . I built this thing . . . very simple. Push a button. Anytime. But I couldn't. I just couldn't. My own family."

He closed his eyes again, he lay with death on his face. Nick looked at the distant white building. Shepherd said, "There's a machine up there. I built it. It's much stronger . . . it will make the ground permanent. No more gate to open. Free for years and years . . . half-life . . . unknown. Goes into the air. But the thing is, you push the button . . . you kill . . . and kill . . . from out of the air."

His eyes were open now. He was softer now, his grip had ended. But the tension had gone from his face. He lay there dreamily, on the edge of sleep, looking at Nick's face like a weary father. He lay his free hand over his heart.

"Always knew they'd come back in. The Huston device was . . . temporary. You see? They could always drop a bomb. But now . . . not now . . . all your choice. Free world. Push the button. All in God's hands. So I built it, and I sat there, in the night, watching the rain. . . ." He closed his eyes. After a moment, eyes still closed, he said softly, "God's hands. I give it to you. Choice. All in God's . . . go on up there and think. It'll go out into the air. It'll go a long way. But it's all yours now . . . the world near here . . . brave new world . . . but I couldn't. Not my own . . . all in God's hands."

He stopped to rest. Nick felt the pulse. Beating. Any moment now. Ruth came with morphine, in shots. Nick said, "He doesn't talk of pain."

"But he's only resting?"

"Yes."

Ruth had pills. No way to give them. A car came up: Nick saw a couple, a man and a woman. Then there was another car, the Jesuit priest. They had heard the explosion. They knew nothing else. They knelt around Shepherd, and Ruth was telling them what happened when Shepherd stopped breathing. The hand was still on Nick's forearm. It loosened; he caught it: no pulse. The face had gone to rest.

Done.

Nick backed away. They saw. They were silent. The priest knelt, began to pray in a soft voice. Nick looked up at the dead tank. Out on the green there were two other bodies. He backed off to a tree and sat down there by himself, and Ruth came and sat next to him and leaned against him and he held her. Had not really known the man. And yet cared. His own family.

God in Heaven.

Choice?

Ruth had heard nothing. No point in telling her. Not now, not yet. He sat looking up at the white building. The message came into his brain, at last, sent by a dying mind. Push the button.

He sat, then stopped thinking. No point in thinking. He'd long ago given up logic: taught by his father. Learn by seeing, learn by waiting, thinking sometimes but not always, wait, and see, and then act when the time comes. When the time comes, you'll know it.

He wanted to see the thing up there: the button. He got up and began to go that way, telling Ruth that there was something Shepherd had told him about that he had to see, and she came with him holding his hand, not knowing about the button, and he did not tell her.

He went up the long stairs to the top of the building. There was no one there. He found the Dietrich Lab, opened white doors.

The thing was a small white house without windows. The long, winding, metal chimney went up to the skylight. All around the white house there were small boxes, most of them empty. There was some wiring coming out of the rear of the house, and it led to a generator, a red round generator that Nick knew: electronic, powerful, complex, simple to start. He walked around the house, which had a fiberglass roof. Ruth was asking him about the thing. He said, "Something Shepherd was building."

He did not tell her what it was. He examined the generator.

There was the button.

In a few seconds: a current. Did the current mean only heat?

The thing that looked like a house had no doors. It had a square sliding vane like a window. Nick did not touch it. He looked up at the thing like a chimney that went out through the skylight. The dust will go into the air.

How far?

He found himself a bare wood table by a window. He could see out across the blasted lawn to the silver tank and the people around the body of Shepherd and the priest by one other body near the building. It was a bright day and there was little wind. And all across town there was still that vast silence, that stillness, toward which the troops were coming.

NINE

The word that Shepherd was dead came in at about two in the afternoon. It was picked up by one of the Team members listening to a police frequency and he interrupted to ask questions and a voice told him that Shepherd was dead. The voice was disturbed, would not identify itself, wanted to know, in innocence, why Shepherd had died, what the tanks were doing there. The Team member brought word to Ring and he went to the radio but he got no answer. Nick Tesla no longer answered, not since he'd shot into the tank. But two men at least were dead. And the man who spoke on the radio said he did not know who Shepherd was, or know about the machine, or know Nick. So he was part of no team. He was only a man alive in the Zone, and he was bitter, the man said, about the tank, and about Shepherd's death, and he could not explain this to him. Ring began to write that down, to send the word to Hiller, and another member of the Team picked up another voice on the radio, another innocent observer. This one turned out to be a priest, who had been waiting, apparently, for God's will to be done, and he wanted an explanation for the killing of Shepherd, but over the radio none could be given, and Ring was called, talked to a bitter priest, and told the man to come out, and when the man refused, told him to stay away from the University, which was dangerous ground. It was a difficult conversation. But the priest confirmed that Shepherd was dead and said that he would perform the funeral service, at the request of others. Ring wanted to know what others, and the priest did not want to talk anymore, excused himself politely, and was gone.

Ring sent the word by plane, not by radio. Hiller would get it in not much more than an hour. He told the Team to keep quiet about it. At about that time the six tanks began to move.

He went out into the warming afternoon and watched them line up single file on the road: big tanks, heavy armor, massive guns. All automatic, altogether; no rifles could hurt them now. Armitage had assembled all the monitors, all the remote drivers, was overseeing it himself, but Ring was executive officer. Ring would order the shooting. The six tanks were in perfect condition and all well fueled and well loaded but not very fast, so that it would take them a while to go down that road and all the way into the town, so it was going to be a long, long afternoon, and Ring stood there while the gate rose, as it had that morning, and the tanks, the empty tanks, went one by one through the gate with the deep thunder of the engines, and Ring stood there watching another attack of this eerie war, the war against an unseen Wall, and knew the tanks would go through it, the tanks were immune, and as he watched them go around the last bend by dark trees and go one by one out of sight behind the trees he felt a crawling chill of a world gone much too far, a world attacking an invisible Wall with empty tanks, that he could aim and fire because he was *there*, remembering at that moment that incredible splendor of the first step down onto the Moon, long ago, wishing he'd been *there*, and felt now useless and outside, motionless, nothing to do now but stand or sit and watch the screen, and move a gadget, and wait, and see the world in there on a little monitor. Well, maybe this afternoon . . . where was Nick?

He sat near Armitage, outside the crammed radio booth. Six monitors: the first looked down that empty road. Ring had seen too much of that; he turned away, looked down the golf course at motionless helicopters.

Armitage said, "Question. What if Nick Tesla shows up with a gun again? Tries to stop the new tanks?"

Ring's mind saw the young face: rage in young eyes. After a moment Ring said, "*Dam*mit."

Armitage nodded. "Yes, sirree. It'd be fairly easy for him to do. The lenses are all vulnerable. And looky here, Shepherd had two friends come out against us. May be some more. What do you think?"

Ring chilled, blinked. Then he said, "If necessary. Do what's necessary."

"Right." Armitage grunted. "I hope to God it ain't necessary. But . . . we need those tanks. And Nick already stopped one of them. I wonder . . . did you expect that?"

"No."

"Me neither." Armitage shrugged, squinted upward. "Beautiful day. For a change. No damned rain. Be rough if it was raining like hell, like it was the other day."

"Any word on the . . . radioactivity?"

"None."

"If this doesn't work."

"Then we hit with Big Brother. *That* will work. Oh, yes."

Ring agreed. But he felt once more that distant black round thing in the back of his brain, rolling again like a waking giant in a bad, bad dream. Then he got a call from Hiller, from Washington . . .

Seattle.

Hiller spoke very quickly. He wanted no long speeches. He thought Ring ought to know. The same disease had broken out there. An hour ago. We were moving that way. Same method. A friend of the man. Must have been a friend of the man. He said, "We've got some of the rest. We've got the machine in Rome, we found it. I gather Shepherd is all right?"

"Yes." Ring lied. "How bad is Seattle?"

"Very bad. Also a little news. Don't know if it's true. Another town in Europe. Somewhere in Austria. Don't know quite where. But it's open warfare now. A crazy revolution. So we'll have to hit. Are you on the move?"

"We're on the move."

"Let me know as soon as it stops. Because if it doesn't stop . . . we have to go nuclear."

Ring hung up.

He went back over to look at the lead monitor. He sat watching the long barrel of the long cannon. Go down the long empty road.

* * *

There were nine people on the lawn below, moving around the red-gray hole that was like a shell hole, moving to see the bodies, and it was a mild shock to see a crowd, after all this quiet time: nine live people, three more dead. Nick did not recognize anyone: the old composer had not come. He did not know how many of these, if any, were Shepherd's friends. He did not know who knew about this machine, or Huston's machine; he watched, waited, but no one went into the long low building across the way; no one looked up toward the window where he sat in silence.

After a while he was almost certain. He was the only one who knew. He remembered Ring's threat of the morning: they could hit here at any moment without warning, with a missile. He looked up at the sky. He thought: you'll never see it coming.

He sat gazing down out of the window, waiting. He had no goal, no plan, no hope, no fear. He was waiting.

Ruth sat near him. After some time he became aware of her, that she was watching him, and he looked at her face and she looked from him to the machine and then back, and he could tell by the wide wonder of her eyes that she was beginning to see. But he said nothing. Not time yet. She went

on watching him without words. He turned back inside
himself. He began to study the rising tubes. Born there:
Shepherd's dust. It will go out into the air. It will blow in the
wind. South and east. How far will it blow?

God knows.

Can't go far. Can't kill many. Can it? God knows. I don't
know. But it will settle to the ground, settle as dust, and
where the dust lies the land will be lethal and almost empty,
almost empty, for a long, long, long, long time.

He remembered: dead babies in the hospital. Rows of
dead babies. Ah. Don't think of that.

He went to the red generator, touched it, trying to swing
his mind into the mechanics of this thing, the technical
difficulties, not . . . the little dead bodies.

He watched the people below gathering covers for the
bodies down there and then drive cars up onto the blasted
lawn and under ruined trees, and begin gathering up the
bodies like dead flowers and taking them away. To burial?
Where? He remembered the priest: like to talk to him. What
does he think now? And then the lawn was empty and the
wind had picked up, and he thought of a burning wind and
watched tufts of blasted leaves ripple and flicker across the
lawn.

Ruth said she was hungry. Nick looked at his watch: 2:15.
He felt no hunger. Ruth said she could run down and pick up
a sandwich or something, mainly something to drink . . . did
he want anything? He said, "Fine, thank you," and she came
to him and said, "Let me clean your face; there's blood on
your face."

She went away for a moment but came back with nothing
because there was no flow of water in the building, and she
said, "Have to go get something wet somewhere." Then she
knelt by him and kissed him on the cheek lightly, gently.

Nick said, "Listen. Why don't you go back to the boat.
Take a run away from this place. Away from here."

215

"I don't want to leave you."

"They may hit this place. Any minute now. There may be a bomb."

"Are you staying?"

"A little while."

"What are you going to do?" She pointed at the generator. She said, "You can turn that on."

"Yes."

"This one is stronger?"

"Yes."

"What are you going to do?"

"I don't know."

"This one is . . . much stronger."

"I think so. If I turn it on . . . they'll leave us alone."

She did not move. He said, "It'll kill a lot of people."

She was motionless: beautiful. He reached out, held her forearm. She stared at him, at the machine. She said, "What do you want me to do?"

"Nothing."

"Can I help you?"

"No."

"What are you going to do?"

"I don't know."

She said no more for a long moment. He sat gazing at her magnificent legs. It came again: vision of dead babies. Rows of dead babies. He groaned. She said, "What can I do?"

He shook his head.

"Let me get something for you. You just sit there and don't you move."

"Okay."

"I'll go down and get you something. What do you want?"

"Take a gun with you this time."

"I don't like pistols. I'll take that rifle. But I'll be all right. But what can I get you? Something to drink?" She gave a tender smile. "It may be time for a drink."

He said, "You want me to push the button?"

She stood for a moment, then moved closer, bent her head. "I don't know."

"I don't think I will. Is that . . . all right with you?"

She said nothing. He couldn't see her face.

"Lassie? They'll be coming back in. Pretty soon. You want me to push the button?"

She said nothing. He put his arm around her; her head came against his chest. Then she pushed back, looked up, gave him a pat on his cheek. She said, "I'll go get you something. What do you want?"

"Anything."

She smiled. She had tears in her eyes. "Anything?"

"Anything."

"I'll be right back." She moved toward the door.

"Take the damned rifle."

She picked it up, looked back. She said, "Maybe we can have a few days. Just a few more days. Will they settle for that?"

"Maybe." But he knew they wouldn't.

She went out the door and down the stairs, and he was alone by the white metal house, the red generator: the black button.

No one below: no one in sight. He was alone.

He walked around the room. He walked around and around.

Blank the mind. Punch the computer: clear the brain. Think not for a while. Vision of dead babies.

To push a button . . . is murder.

Quite possibly a missile is coming my way, at this moment.

Daddy used to say, "When the first missile is dropped, and it's coming, it's coming, I hope the damned thing comes right down my chimney."

If I were out there and knew what was in here I'd push my button.

Don't want to kill anybody.

Never did.

I don't hate anybody.

I don't love anybody.

He stopped by the black button. Very simple. All you really do, really, *my God in Heaven,* is push one button. Is that all? Must be all. He knelt, marveled. The choice of fate. The power in that little thing. So easy. Like all the great weapons, just press the delicate trigger. He put his finger down, caressed the cold button. Many gauges. Well made.

I don't hate anybody.

I feel . . . tired.

He sat in the vision of the rows of dead babies. One had lived. He thought: if I stay in this town, and the town goes on being empty, how do I ever go back in that hospital and look at all the little skeletons? He closed his eyes.

No more of that.

I can't do that.

No more dead babies.

So.

All done.

He sat for a moment without thinking of anything at all: empty in the brain. Then he heard once more the coming of the tank.

More than one. A blossoming roar.

He went to the window.

They came one by one out into the sunlight, out from the dark of the trees. There were six of them. The first came out into the center of the lawn and stopped, swung, facing the building across the way where the man named Huston had built the first machine, which was blazing now, sending out a separate message. The first tank was the leader, with eyes, but they all must have eyes, they were all moving into position facing the building across the way, six tanks in a long slight curve, all the cannon lifting, aiming, zeroing in. Then for a moment there was no motion and Nick thought of the hand somewhere pressing buttons now, and then out of the corner of his eye he saw movement and turned and saw the tank of the morning, the tank that had killed Shepherd, the tank that had seemed dead but had only been blinded, unable to move because it couldn't see; that tank was moving now, coming into position on the far right guided by the new eyes in the new tanks that were guided in turn by the man somewhere with the buttons. Nick heard no clear words. Must be the last threat. He sat waiting. Long silence. No motion. They did not wait long. Blast from the central tank: blossom from the wall. Smoke blew away: he saw a round hole in red brick. He had not known where Huston's office was. But the tank knew. Another blast: a white blossom, flicks of flying brick. Two more in rapid succession, one slightly to the right. One tank was in motion now; position farther to the right: to see inside? Two more bloomed side by side: the hole was widening. He saw whiteness, something flat white: concrete. The shooting went on. He turned his eyes away and looked at the white house with the flat square windows and across the tubing to the red generator. Looking at his watch, did not notice the time. But after a few moments the firing down there will pierce the wall and go through and break the machine, stop the machine.

Nick backed away from the window.

Don't want to watch that.

Let it be, let it be.

Time to get out of here.

Ruth.

Will come back through the tanks?

Message: *she's carrying a rifle.*

He ran to the window.

They wouldn't shoot.

She'll come running. If she comes around the side.

He tried to open the window. All he could see was blots of

smoke. But he saw her coming. He saw the blue dress under a tree on the far side: running. He couldn't open the window. He started to yell. The sound of the guns was huge. She came running this way, cupping the rifle, coming through smoke. No time. Nick screamed. She was running across uneven ground toward the door down below and she stumbled in the dirt and came up kneeling, rifle in her hands, and Nick saw the near tank turn, the machine-gun turret swivel; he screamed and banged the glass, Ruth came on running, came down below him out of sight in blowing smoke, and the machine gun blinked, firing, quick burst, flutter, quick burst. No sight of Ruth. Nick ran to the door, blocking the mind, blocking the blinded mind: she came away, she got away, God help us, she came in through the door—and at the bottom of the stairs she lay on the floor face down. Blood on the floor below her. Blood coming out. Blood on the back of the dress. Went right through her. He got down, took hold, turned the lovely girl, saw blood on the mouth, blood on the cheek, eyes opening but already gone, but she saw him, her eyes moved: she put out a hand and touched his cheek. He said something, did not know what he said, looked at the bloodied dress, oh why, why, oh absent God, and she said softly, a wounded voice, very softly, "Saint Nick." She closed her eyes. Went to sleep. He knew. He put her down. He knelt there and began to cry. He had not cried since he was a very small boy, and the tears were hot all over his face. Like the blood down there. All the blood down there. *Goddamn them. Goddamn them.*

The rage blossomed. He patted her face, went on crying. He stood up. He said loudly, "You did it once too often." He turned, went up the stairs, looked back down, saw the dead body, yelled, roared: "Goddamn you all! You did it once too often!"

He ran back up the stairs to the room where the button was waiting. He sat there slowing himself while the guns blazed on outside, below, wrecking the other building. He studied the machine, learned what to do, opened the gauges, pressed the button. He heard a soft hum. He examined the fuel tank: the generator would last for hours. The hum increased in strength, like a tone of whining music. The thing was calm and quiet and still cold. There was the beginning of a flutter on the wall of the white metal building but it smoothed, and the sound was drowned in the sound of the guns.

He left the building and went away under the trees. He was going down toward the river, back to the boat, but he stopped and began to cry. He sat down under a tree until the guns stopped firing and it was quiet. Then he wiped his eyes and stared up at the sky, the clear blue sky, and then got up and started walking out to the airport and the airplanes.

*   *   *

At 3:46 that afternoon the radiation stopped.

There were meters all around the Zone, meters that picked up that signal from the center, and at 3:46 the last necessary shot from an unmanned tank went through the wall of the Physics Lab and stopped the Huston machine. The signal ended. Whoops and howls went all around the line, cheers of a successful football crew, and Ring gave the Team his signal to go in. The Team was one crew of one helicopter: they would fly as far in as possible, back into that Zone, and if they detected no more radiation Ring would follow, with Armitage, in a flock of new copters. It was a long, pleasant, swelling moment. Some of the troops were hopping up and down, and Ring stood by the last gate on the black road that led into the Zone, slowly punching one flat palm with a round fist, still waiting, peering down that empty road into that empty country, watching the first test copter zoom down the road like a slow happy eagle, sending back cheery messages. No radiation. Ring's copter was warming. Armitage was patting him on the shoulder.

"This going to be interesting, damned interesting, ha? What do you think? Goddamn!"

Men were congratulating each other. One aide told Ring something about a press release now being necessary; another handed Ring a black hand radio: Hiller. Ring moved off by himself. Hiller said, "I hear your radiation's off. That right? Goddamn. Good job. Damn glad to hear that. Listen, if you were up *here* . . . listen, you going in? Be careful. When are you going in?"

"Few minutes. I'll give the boys time to tell me if it's clean."

"Well, it may not be clean."

"What?"

"That thing out in Seattle is a mess. But yours is all right. Thank God for that. We're holding our own."

"Holding our own?"

"We'll get 'em, dammit. One by one, but we'll get 'em. But that damn thing in Seattle, I tell you, it's scared hell out of people around here. Me included. I tell you."

"What's happening?"

A small cold chill. Ring thought: you never know all of it. Bits and pieces, one fleck at a time. He sensed something enormous. Hiller told him not to worry. Ring swore. Hiller said, "Okay, buddy, I'll level. The thing out in Seattle has no center. It's not round. You follow me? We don't know where to hit. We'll find it, hell yes, but we just don't know." Hiller's voice quit. Ring sensed genuine fear. Hiller said, "We're keepin' it quiet, Christ, you must know that, but the goddamn thing . . ."

"Go on and tell me."

"Okay, okay. The damn thing is drifting. It's on the move, like a dust cloud. It's coming slowly east. What do you think of that, ha? Goddamn. It's coming like a cold front. Killed a hell of a lot of people already and we don't know what to do—what the hell can we do? We can't even release information. People will run like hell, but if we stay shut up, I'll tell you, even the boss . . . wait a minute."

Long moment of silence. Ring looked south. Copter out of sight. Everyone here overjoyed. No bad news on the radio. Ring waited, waited. Cold front. Coming east. Ring called Hiller. In a moment, a strange voice: "Shouldn't have told you. But what the hell. Listen, whatever they turned on in Seattle is not like the old machine. It puts radioactive dust into the air and the damned stuff is drifting with the wind. No way to stop that. No way at all. But, it can't drift far. It'll settle out. Fall out, sure. It'll go for a way and then fall, so it may kill a hell of a lot of people, but it can't do that for long, Jesus, I hope . . ."

Ring sat with the black box in his hand. He looked west: high thin cloud. Corelli had said: *it's a war.* And Corelli was afraid. Ring looked down the empty road. Gate now open. He heard: a sudden silence. He looked: over by the radio equipment men were quieting, listening. Ring thought: *it's a war.*

A war . . . down an empty road.

His radio began again. Not Hiller's voice: a voice unknown. "Mr. Ring, are you there?"

"Yes. This is Ring."

"Situation here rather serious. Has your radiation there ceased? *Entirely?*"

"Yes. I've sent in Team One." At that moment Ring saw astounded faces listening to the radio signals from Team One. The unknown voice said to Ring, "Good. Quick as I can, I'll . . . well. The thing we found in Rome, the thing that quit last night because of power failure, that thing is a small machine. We want you to get right in and find the one you've stopped. Main thing you have to know is this: the thing you'll find is very simple, it needs only *heat* to work. Got that? Heat. So as soon as you get in there, you'll find some sort of heat generator. I don't mean just a simple oven-type thing, no, but something that created a temperature of several thousand degrees. Now, keep an . . . just a moment."

The voice stopped. Armitage was coming this way. Ring knew.

Ring said, into the radio, "Hello? Hello?"

Armitage said, "The Team is coming back out."

"How bad is it?"

Armitage shook his head: face bewildered. Ring said, "Strong radiation right? Where does it begin?"

"Near the center."

"What else do you know?"

Armitage shook his head. Ring swore at the black radio. He moved to the Team radio zone. There were men sitting and standing with headphones on, open-mouthed. Ring asked questions. One man said, wide-eyed, "Sir, they're picking it up in the south, too. Down south of here, on the other side."

Armitage picked up a headphone. The voice on Ring's radio came back. He plucked it up, listened. It was again Hiller, tight and high: ". . . not much time, but what the hell. You wanna know, old buddy, so I'll tell you. Shepherd's friends are on the move. We didn't get there in time. Now it's two. One in Seattle, one in Denver. The stuff is going into the wind. We got nothing to hit. Nothing. Any suggestions? You're the old war hero. What we need right now is a war hero. Any suggestions?"

"Denver. Somebody turned the thing on in Denver?"

"Yup. Only this one is different. It drifts in the wind. It's coming this way, sport. How does that grab you? We have, oh what the hell, we can fly out of here. But the point is, there's silence in other places, two places in Europe, one in Russia, altogether: six. All over the world. The damned stuff is in the air, buster. What the hell. What do I do now?"

"Sir?" To Ring, face of a young Captain. "Radiation is

intense, and moving. Moving, sir. Report from the south. Ah, sir, what do you advise?"

He wanted the reply of nuclear attack. Ring turned away.

Hiller was saying, ". . . get out of here, I guess. Do the best you can. Goddamn it, there's no center. How the hell can we hit anything if there's no center? But if we don't hit . . . it'll go around the world."

Ring stood there, radio in hand, faces watching him. Hiller said, "Oh, my God!"

"What?"

Silence. Faces were pale. In a moment, Hiller said, "I'll see you, Dick. Do the best you can. What the hell, maybe. You never know. But me, I don't go for any damned shelter. Not me. So. Take it easy, sport. See you around."

Ring put down the black radio. He was calm; had learned this moment long ago as a combat commander. He asked for a detailed statement from Armitage's senior officer. He stood waiting; heard copter blades, saw Team One coming back up the road. It landed on the golf course. Some troops were running that way. A Major came to Ring, saluted: a gray-faced Major, a slight mustache. He said, "Radioactivity is intense near the center, is moving west and south, as if pushed by the wind. Is not coming this way. But if the wind changes . . . it moves with wind speed: ten to fifteen knots."

At that moment Ring knew: it was going around the world.

Cold front.

He looked at the black radio. He knew Hiller was gone. No more word from the top. Too late. But then, there was never much word from the top.

Ring walked away from the group by the radios. He sat by himself on the railing of a fence in the calm, warm, quiet afternoon.

Radiation out there . . . will come this way. Cold front. A matter of time.

How much time?

Hours.

Maybe a few days.

Corelli knew . . . the man would win.

Ring was amazed. He sat there shaking his head.

We lost the war.

Nothing to hit. Nowhere to go.

I don't like shelters myself.

Ring took out a cigarette, lighted it, puffed into the sky.

Nick Tesla—is alive in there.

Wonder why.

But . . . you never know the answers, Richard. The whole damn thing, from beginning to end, is a mystery. Begins as mystery, ends as mystery, is ending now, with the wind from the west.

And he did not even think of running. He sat there smoking.

Armitage came up. No one had told Armitage the rest of it. There would be no wide reports. But the stuff was coming, out there, like a cold front, a cold front across the world, and Ring had thought nuclear war inevitable anyway, only a matter of time, so he could take this calmly, smoking a cigarette on a warm afternoon, feeling the breeze from the west, slowly turning his mind toward that country behind that Wall, beginning to think about the thing that was alive in there, alive, Nick Tesla . . . but Armitage wanted orders.

Ring said, "There's nothing to do."

He told Armitage to withdraw. The wind was coming. No point in thinking any more about that. Ring sat alone, looking down the road. A few of the helicopters took off and flew out, headed north. Ring saw: Corelli.

The little man came up this way, hands in his pockets. He had aged a good deal in the night. But he was at peace. They stood side by side for a long while without speaking. On the road beyond them the soldiers were grouping to withdraw. After a long, aging silence Ring said, "How long do you think it'll take?"

"Oh, I don't know."

"Well, we've got until sundown here. Hm." Ring chuckled. "It sure is a peaceful war, isn't it, when it comes this way?"

"Well, the last few minutes . . ." Corelli put his hand to his mouth.

"Comes like a cold front. Will move . . . over all the earth. How long do you think that'll take?"

"The thing is spreading now, all over the world."

"It won't take long."

"No."

"Hm." Ring shook his head. "So the armies don't matter anymore."

Out on the road the troops were piling into the truck line, beginning to move north. Ring thought: a few more hours. Cigarette done: he took out another. He put out his hand, touched the metal gate: the gate that Shepherd refused to open. He said, "It'll go all over the world. Right?"

Corelli nodded. Ring said, "No way to stop it. It just moves with the wind."

"Yes."

"So. There'll be no more gates."

"What?" Corelli was shielding his eyes.

"I mean, all over the earth, no more borders anymore. No more guards at the borders."

A marvelous thought. In his mind, Ring saw empty gates, unguarded fences, unmanned guns: everywhere. He shook his head, awed. He said, "But there'll be a few people. Hm. You know, old friend, that's the one thing I never expected. I always knew it would be empty, someday. But now . . . all over the world . . . just a few . . . everywhere."

Corelli had tears in his eyes.

Ring said, "How many you think there'll be?"

Corelli shook his head.

Ring said, "Odds are about two thousand to one. So there'll be quite a few. Here and there, in the big cities, a few hundred. Hm. What do you think of that?"

Corelli said nothing.

Ring said, "Gee, I'd like to see that."

"Me, too," Corelli said.

"A few people. Everywhere. Hm. I wonder what kind of world . . . I guess they'll begin again, don't you think?"

"I don't know."

"They'll have to. But I wonder . . . what kind of man is in there."

"So do I."

"Is he *that* different, from you and me?"

"I hope so." Corelli crossed himself.

Ring said slowly, "Only a few. I'll bet you, in a little while, they'll talk over radios. And they'll use only one language."

Corelli had turned, was beginning to walk away.

"Where you going?"

"To pray."

Ring nodded.

Corelli said, "Want to come with me?"

Ring shook his head.

"Goodbye," Corelli said.

He walked up the road to the north.

Ring had a staff car on the road near him, a gray staff car, like the one Nick Tesla had used. He walked over to that one, opened the door, sat there. It was now very quiet, the troops had gone, there was little wind. Ring sat approaching sleep. He would not miss anything. He had not lost anything. The world out there had no strong dreams. But the world yet to come . . . oh, if I could see that.

Ring put his hands on the wheel, touched the starter.

The gate was open.

It was late in the afternoon: not long until sundown.

Ring started the engine.

Brave new world. What kind of man? You may live long enough to see . . . the beginning.

Odds: 2,000 to 1.

He began to drive forward.

A few men alive on that ground up ahead. They'll begin again. Will they repeat the old, the bloody world? Will the new world be better? Or will it be worse?

God only knows.

Ring drove through the Wall.